"I was rude and the

A smile flickered at the ed[...]
That's true."

Vernon managed a playful grin. "I'm glad we agree."

Sadie's smile widened. "Me, too."

Vernon felt his throat tighten. He sensed something growing between them, something more than a friendship between an employer and his children's nanny.

"Vernon?"

The sound of his name on her lips sent a strange feeling through him. *"Ya?"*

"Did you mean what you said? That just because something is different from how it's always been done doesn't mean it's bad?"

"Ya. I meant it."

"Not many other Amish folk around here think that way."

"Maybe not. But there are plenty of things that make me different from most of the others."

Sadie's brow crinkled. "Like what?"

"Nothing. I should go." No one else was responsible for his wife's death or his sister's disability. Vernon was different in a way that could never be forgiven.

Whatever bond had begun to form between them, Vernon had to sever it. Sadie deserved far better than he could ever give.

After **Virginia Wise**'s oldest son left for college and her youngest son began high school, she finally had time to pursue her dream of writing novels. Virginia dusted off the keyboard she once used as a magazine editor and journalist to create a world that combines her love of romance, family and Plain living. Virginia loves to wander Lancaster County's Amish country to find inspiration for her next novel. While home in Northern Virginia, she enjoys painting, embroidery, taking long walks in the woods, and spending time with family, friends and her husband of almost twenty-five years.

Books by Virginia Wise

Love Inspired

An Amish Christmas Inheritance
The Secret Amish Admirer
Healed by the Amish Nanny

Visit the Author Profile page at LoveInspired.com for more titles.

Healed by the Amish Nanny

VIRGINIA WISE

LOVE INSPIRED

INSPIRATIONAL ROMANCE

If you purchased this book without a cover you should be aware
that this book is stolen property. It was reported as "unsold and
destroyed" to the publisher, and neither the author nor the
publisher has received any payment for this "stripped book."

LOVE INSPIRED®

INSPIRATIONAL ROMANCE

Recycling programs
for this product may
not exist in your area.

ISBN-13: 978-1-335-59745-8

Healed by the Amish Nanny

Copyright © 2024 by Virginia Wise

All rights reserved. No part of this book may be used or reproduced in
any manner whatsoever without written permission except in the case of
brief quotations embodied in critical articles and reviews.

This is a work of fiction. Names, characters, places and incidents are either the
product of the author's imagination or are used fictitiously. Any resemblance
to actual persons, living or dead, businesses, companies, events or locales is
entirely coincidental.

For questions and comments about the quality of this book, please contact us
at CustomerService@Harlequin.com.

® is a trademark of Harlequin Enterprises ULC.

Love Inspired
22 Adelaide St. West, 41st Floor
Toronto, Ontario M5H 4E3, Canada
www.LoveInspired.com

Printed in Lithuania

MIX
Paper | Supporting
responsible forestry
FSC® C021394

He healeth the broken in heart,
and bindeth up their wounds.
—*Psalm* 147:3

To Aunt Joy, the artist in our family. You forged your own path in life and inspired me to forge my own.

Chapter One

Sadie Lapp's fingers tightened around the handle of her suitcase as she stared up at the large, foreboding farmhouse. Dark, peeling paint clung to the weather-beaten walls and shutters. Overgrown hedges blocked the first-floor windows. Sadie listened to the sound of hoofbeats fading in the distance as the bishop's horse and buggy slowly wound down the country road, away from her. She turned her head and watched him disappear over a faraway hill, surrounded by sweeping fields of golden wheat and yellow feed corn.

She was alone with strangers now.

Well, not strangers, exactly. Vernon Kauffman and his family were members of the church district, but they never mingled on church Sundays after the service. And they never dropped in on anyone on visiting Sundays. The widower, along with his three children and sister, kept to himself, isolated on his farm at the far edge of the district, away from any neighbors.

A muggy July breeze ruffled the cornstalks in the field beside the house, whipped against Sadie's purple cape dress, and sent a wave through the dead, brown grass. She hugged herself as a chill ran down her spine. The wind died down, leaving the farmyard still and silent. Not even the chickens were out. She felt like she had come to the edge of the world.

Sadie frowned and forced herself to take a step toward the front door. She was being silly. Hadn't she been the one who had insisted on taking a job? Of course, she had never intended to work for the Kauffmans, that was certainly sure. Vernon's dark eyes and hard expression intimidated her, and she had always felt relieved that he didn't come round on visiting Sundays.

Maybe her *daed* had been right. He had warned her it wouldn't be easy to move away from home for a job, even if she was headstrong and full of spirit. In fact, it was that headstrong spirit that had gotten her in this mess in the first place. She had longed for her life to begin and had jumped at the first chance to get away from home. She had pushed her father, Abram, until he relented.

"I won't allow you to work for the *Englisch* under any circumstances," Abram had insisted, but eventually he agreed that Sadie could become a live-in nanny for a good Amish family—if Bishop Amos approved. "Young girls shouldn't leave home at all," Abram had said with an exasperated sigh. "But if you won't hear reason and insist on running off to find work, then you have to go through the bishop. He'll make sure you go to a *gut* Amish household where you'll be under a godly, watchful eye."

"But, *Daed*, I'm twenty-two years old," Sadie had pointed out. "That isn't so young. And I'm doing this because we need the money. I'm trying to help our family. I'm not running off. I'm being responsible, ain't so?" Sadie had been responsible for so long that sometimes she felt she might burst. She had looked after her six younger siblings since she was old enough to tie a shoelace. Now that her younger sister had grown up enough to take Sadie's place, Sadie saw a chance to help her family in a new way—a way that might give her a little more freedom. But her *daed* sure didn't see it that way.

Abram's eyes had narrowed when she pointed out these facts. His fingers had run through his long salt-and-pepper beard as he studied her. "We both know you've got a wayward spirit about you, what with all that artistic nonsense that you do."

"But the bishop approves of my paintings. He says they don't go against the *Ordnung*. I don't sign them or seek attention for them. And the money I get from selling them at the Millers' gift shop has helped our family."

Abram had grunted as his fingers kept sliding through his beard. Sadie had shifted in her chair under her father's long, hard stare. A moment had passed before Abram had spoken again. "Like I said, Bishop Amos will send you to a *gut* family. They'll keep you on the straight and narrow. Otherwise they'll send you back to us. If that happens, you can be sure I'll keep you on the right path."

Sadie had swallowed all the words she wanted to say. She knew they would be wasted on her father. Instead, she would let the frustration flow into her next painting. The colors would be bright red, the paint strokes jagged. *"Oll recht, Daed,"* she had murmured, then shut her mouth tightly before the words she really wanted to say slipped out.

Sadie had not been able to contain her excitement after the decision was made that she could get a job. Her heart had knocked around her chest for the next three days, until the bishop showed up on the doorstep of her family's yellow farmhouse. "You've found me something?" Sadie had asked, her heart flip-flopping faster than ever.

"Ya." The bishop had smiled at her as he took off his straw hat and scratched the bald spot on his head. He was a

small, wizened man and Sadie had to look down at him to meet his eyes, which crinkled at the corners as he grinned. "Vernon Kauffman has need of you."

That was when Sadie's excitement disappeared as quickly as a bucket of kitchen scraps thrown in the pigpen.

"*Ach, nee*, I couldn't. He's…" Sadie had looked away, embarrassed to think so badly of an Amish brother.

"I know he's not the friendliest sort, but that won't keep him from being a *gut* employer. He's a *gut* man, even if he does have some unusual ways about him." Bishop Amos had looked amused then and added, "Maybe you two will see eye to eye, *ya*? After all, you don't think like everyone else around here either, *ain't so*?"

"Being an artist is different than being a—" Sadie had cut herself off. That sentence was not going to end well.

"A recluse?" Bishop Amos had cocked his head and looked at her, waiting for her to say more.

Sadie had wanted to say, *a strange man who makes me feel like he can see right through me*. Instead she had shaken her head. "I just don't know if it's a *gut* fit, that's all." Her eyes darted to her father. Surely he would back her up. Hadn't he wanted to keep her at home, under his supervision, in the first place?

But instead, Abram had nodded thoughtfully. "I trust your judgement on this, Amos. Vernon runs a *gut* household. And his sister, Arleta, is a stickler for the rules. They aren't a friendly sort, that's certain sure, but they will keep a close eye on my Sadie. She won't go astray."

Bishop Amos slapped his straw hat against his thigh. "*Gut*. I'm glad we can all agree on this. I am certain sure it will be for the best." He gave Sadie a reassuring glance. "For everyone."

Sadie's mother, Ada, had been just as hesitant as Sadie

but would never question her husband or the bishop. So she had sent Sadie away with a new quilt, a sandwich wrapped in wax paper and a Bible verse written in careful cursive on a scrap of paper. *God is with you wherever you go*, it read. Her mother's lip had trembled as they hugged good-bye and her arms squeezed tighter than ever before, but the only thing she said was, "*Danki*. You have always sacrificed for this family. Just keep following the rules and you'll be *oll recht*."

At the last moment her father had stepped up to the buggy and put a steady hand on Sadie's arm. "You'll do well and…" His deep brown eyes had flickered with emotion that Sadie rarely saw, and she knew her father was struggling to remain stoic. He cleared his throat, looked away and added gruffly, "And I'm proud of you, *dochder*." Then he gave the horse a gentle slap on the rump. "Git on, now," he said to the mare before quickly turning on his heels and striding back toward the farmhouse. Sadie's father rarely spoke well of her; seeing a glimmer of how much he cared beneath his tough, no-nonsense exterior had given her the strength to face the unknown road ahead.

After the long buggy ride to the far outskirts of Bluebird Hills, that conversation with her family felt a lifetime away. And now, standing in the overgrown grass of the Kauffman's empty farmyard, Sadie didn't want to think of her family anymore. As claustrophobic as her home made her feel—there was never any privacy, and always another chore to get done—she wished with all her might to be back in that yellow farmhouse, safe and sound with all the familiar annoyances.

Sadie took a deep breath and forced one foot in front of the other until she reached the front steps of the Kauffman house. Her black athletic shoes slapped against each worn stair, echoing into the silence. When she reached the wide, wraparound porch, the wooden floorboards creaked beneath her weight. She wondered where everyone was. Shouldn't they have come out to greet her?

Sadie swallowed hard, smoothed her apron, straightened her prayer *kapp* and knocked on the front door.

Vernon Kauffman saw the trail of dust billowing up from the long, winding dirt road that led to his house. He paused, leaned against his pitchfork and stared into the distance. The new nanny had arrived. No one else would show up at his farm at this hour—or any hour, for that matter. The rest of the church district had given up on him long ago. And that was just fine with him.

Vernon squinted into the sun as he studied the slow-moving buggy headed away from his land, back toward the heart of Bluebird Hills. He couldn't make out the features of the girl who had stepped out of it, nor did he want to. Better she had never come. He shook his head and readjusted his grip on the pitchfork. Best get back to work. No need to stand and stare. She wouldn't last long anyway. It wouldn't take much time before he scared her away, like all the other nannies. Not intentionally, of course. He had no ill will toward any of them. Thankfully, Bishop Amos must have recognized this, since he was giving the Kauffman family another chance with a new nanny. But Vernon didn't expect anything to be different this time. Young women didn't take to him for some reason. Maybe it was his refusal to chat and smile like other men did when they wanted to put someone at ease. He didn't see the need to coddle anyone, no matter their age or disposition. Small talk and fake smiles didn't put food on the table or clothes on his children's backs. All it did was raise people's expectations—which he would surely disappoint.

Maybe, if he were lucky, this nanny would understand the value of quiet and solitude, just like he did. Unlikely. But he could always hope. And, if he were really lucky, she would be meek and unquestioning, a *gut* Amish girl who wouldn't bother him and could fit into his household without much fuss. Surely *Gott* knew that was what he needed and would send it his way. Being left alone wasn't too much to ask, was it?

His wife had been a *gut*, upright Amish girl. She had been perfect for him—taciturn and stern. Someone who followed rules and never questioned the predictable rhythms of life. Everyone had known where they stood with her and what to expect. Vernon threw a pitchfork of alfalfa hay into the wagon and frowned. He didn't want to think about Lorna. He never wanted to think about her again. So he emptied his mind of everything but the warmth of the sun, the itchy heat of his straw hat against his forehead and the buzz of an insect circling near his ear. But the sharp ache in his chest remained.

That ache never went away, no matter how hard he worked to shove it aside.

A door slammed in the distance. Vernon's eyes moved across a yellow-green cornfield to the *dawdi haus* sitting in the shadow of the farmhouse. Arleta's silhouette filled the doorway, hands on hips. He couldn't make out his older sister's expression from this distance, but he could imagine it. Her eyes would be narrowed, her lips tight. She didn't want a new nanny on the farm any more than he did. But what choice did they have? Arleta couldn't take care of his children after she'd been injured in the buggy accident that killed his wife.

Arleta's face turned toward the fields and Vernon could feel her eyes on him, hard and unyielding. He could feel the blame radiating from that look, even though he could not see her clearly. He knew her well enough to know what she was feeling.

His family had been destroyed by his careless decision to take them out on icy roads. He would live with the consequences for the rest of his life. Vernon turned back to his pitchfork, his expression stoic. He was getting exactly what he deserved. In the distance, he heard the *dawdi haus* door slam shut again and knew Arleta had gone back inside without greeting the new nanny. He would have to try to make the young woman feel welcome on his own, hard as that would be.

"Daed?" a small voice called out. Vernon's heart constricted at the sweet, innocent sound. A moment later, his five-year-old daughter skipped out from the long rows of sweet corn, scampered into the field of freshly mowed alfalfa and looked up at him with a smile. Her apron and face were smudged with dirt.

"You shouldn't be in the fields alone," Vernon said. If Lorna were still alive, she would be keeping an eye on the girl to make sure she was safe.

Lydia's grin disappeared and she looked down. "I wanted to see you."

"You'll see me at supper time," Vernon said, keeping his hands on his pitchfork. He wanted to reach out and pull her into a bear hug. But she looked so small and vulnerable that he didn't trust himself not to cry. He had been holding his feelings in for so long that he knew the smallest act of love might break him. The best thing for Lydia was to see that her father was tough and resilient. Wouldn't that make her feel safe after the loss she had endured?

Lydia kicked a clod of dirt with her toe. "I want to go down to the creek today. I thought maybe you could come with me." Her big brown eyes darted up to his with a hopeful expression.

Vernon resisted the urge to drop his pitchfork, take her hand and head for the creek right then. He shook his head. *"Nee*. I've got to finish my work before sundown."

"But all you ever do is work, *Daed*."

"It's the Amish way, ain't so?"

"Ya." Lydia frowned and kicked another clod of dirt with her bare foot. "But the other *daeds* go swimming with their *kinner*."

Vernon sighed. *"Ya*, well, maybe another time."

"Don't you want to spend time with me, *Daed*?"

Vernon froze. How could he put the storm of emotions inside of him into words that a child would understand? He cleared his throat and looked away. "Of course I want to spend time with you. It's just not possible right now."

Vernon motioned toward the farmyard with his chin. "See that *fraa* over there?"

Lydia nodded.

"She's your new *kinnsmaad*. Go on and say hello. She'll take care of you."

Lydia's brow crinkled and she looked back at her father. "I'd rather go to the creek with you."

Vernon frowned and turned back to his work. "Like I said, I'll see you at supper time."

He didn't watch Lydia leave, but he could hear her little bare feet pounding the dirt as she scampered away. He forced his attention onto the job at hand and told himself he was doing the right thing.

Sadie heard footsteps slap the bare earth and turned to see a small, skinny child with big brown eyes and a button nose galloping out of the wheat field and into the farmyard.

She stepped back from the front door and trotted down the porch steps to meet the girl. "Hello!" Sadie shouted in a voice loud enough to carry across the overgrown hedges and chicken coops.

"Are you my new *kinnsmaad*?" The child pushed a tangled strand of dark blond hair from her face and tried to stuff it under her *kapp*.

"Ya," Sadie said and flashed a relieved grin. "You must be Lydia."

Lydia put her hands on her hips and cocked her head. "How did you know?"

"Bishop Amos told me a *gut* little *maedel* lives here."

"Ya!" Lydia's eyes brightened. "That's me!"

Sadie glanced over Lydia's head. "Where are the grown-ups? I knocked on the door but nobody answered."

"Daed is in the fields. He's always out in the fields. He works all the time."

Sadie's attention moved to the overgrown hedges lining the house. Vernon might be working all day, but he wasn't taking care of the yard, that was certain sure. Sadie knew she shouldn't judge, but it was hard not to. She reminded herself that running a farm alone would be more than enough to keep a man busy, especially with three children and a disabled sister to care for. "Lydia, where are your *brudres* and your *aenti*?"

Lydia shrugged. "I don't know where Ned and Newt are. And *Aenti* Arleta is probably in the *dawdi haus*. She doesn't leave it much."

"Newt?"

"His real name is Jonathon, but he'll only answer to Newt. *Daed* gets frustrated about it sometimes."

"Ya." Sadie stifled a smile. "Unusual nickname."

"It fits him," Lydia said in a matter-of-fact tone, then

slipped her hand in Sadie's. Sadie warmed at the soft, sticky touch. She could feel a layer of grime on the girl's palm but didn't mind. Lydia was a sweet girl who clearly needed more attention. Sadie was beginning to understand why the bishop had sent her here.

"Why don't you show me around?" Sadie asked.

"Oll recht," Lydia said, then continued to chatter as if they had always known one another. "Ned is a nickname for Nathaniel. He would have been called Nate, but there were already three other Nates in the family." Lydia began count-ing off with her free hand. "A first cousin, a second cousin and a great-uncle." She held up three fingers. "That's three whole Nates. It was too confusing. So he's called Ned."

Sadie nodded. "That happens a lot in Amish families, ain't so? We like to use the same names."

Lydia nodded. Her expression looked like she consid-ered herself an expert in the matter. *"Ya.* We only have one other Sadie though, and she moved to Indiana."

"We don't have any. I get to be the only Sadie in my family."

"Does that make you lonely?"

Sadie giggled. "What a funny question." Then she stopped smiling and shook her head. "Not a bad question, you under-stand. It's a *gut* one, just a funny one."

Lydia nodded again. "I understand. I like to be funny, but I'm not as *gut* at it as my *brudres."*

"I'm looking forward to meeting them."

Lydia made a face.

Sadie wondered about Lydia's reaction, but thought it was best to ignore it. "To answer your question, I like being the only Sadie in my family. I feel like I'm kind of differ-ent from the rest of them, so it makes sense."

Lydia led Sadie around the corner of the farmhouse, still holding tight to her hand.

"How are you different?" Lydia asked. "You look the same as everyone else." She squinted up at Sadie. "Except you're prettier than most people. Your eyes are really blue. But *Aenti* Arleta says it isn't *gut* to be pretty. It's *gut* to be Plain."

Sadie thought about it as they stepped over a cracked, overturned flowerpot. "*Ach*, I'm not talking about looks." But Sadie's father had warned her that a man with bad intentions might single her out because she was pretty and had such a *gut*, trusting heart. *You have to be shrewd*, he had said.

Even so, Sadie knew her looks were not what defined her. "I guess what I meant is that I see things in the world that other people don't."

"Like what?" Lydia asked

Sadie pointed upward. "What do you see up there, in the sky?"

"Um…" Lydia scrunched up her face. "Clouds?"

Sadie smiled and her eyes took on a faraway look. "*Ya*. But I also see a unicorn running toward a waterfall." She motioned to a clump of puffy white clouds floating in a field of blue. "See, there…" Her hand swept across the sky. "And there?"

"Mmm." Lydia's face scrunched up a little tighter. "Maybe."

Sadie laughed. "You can see whatever you want in the clouds. Maybe you see something else."

Lydia looked from the sky to Sadie. "Seeing stuff in the clouds makes you different?"

"*Nee*. But seeing lots of things in our everyday world that other people don't does. In the *Englisch* world they call it being an artist. We just call it being different."

"Lydia doesn't need to hear anything about the *Englisch* world," a stern male voice said.

Sadie jerked her attention from the sky to see Vernon Kauffman standing in front of her, holding a jug. They had reached a water pump beside a sprawling red barn and Sadie hadn't even noticed. She always had her head in the clouds—this time literally. "*Nee.* I didn't mean… Of course she doesn't… What I meant—"

Vernon stared at Sadie as she sputtered to a stop and stood still as a statue, staring back at him. His eyes were so dark that Sadie felt she could slip into them and sink into oblivion. He did not blink or flinch. He just kept staring. Sadie was the first to look away. Her gaze shifted back and forth across the farmyard, trying to find a comfortable place to rest.

But those dark eyes drew her back again and her gaze returned to the man's face. She realized it was a handsome face, even though it was weathered and defined by sharp lines and hard angles. The jawline was pronounced, the nose Roman. Sadie had never been this close to Vernon and she certainly had never studied his face before. She noticed her heart was beating fast and she took a step back. Standing so close to him stirred strange feelings in her that she couldn't understand. Was it fear? Intimidation? No, it was something else that she had no name for. And the strangest thing about it was that she didn't want to stop feeling it. Perhaps it was because she had never met anyone who could stare like that—so cold and aloof, but without any hint of cruelty.

Vernon sighed and screwed the lid onto his water jug. "I guess we can't expect any better. No other *kinnsmaad* will work here anymore."

"I am a plenty *gut* worker, Vernon," Sadie said as she raised her chin in response to the insinuation that she was lacking.

He just stared at her with a look that seemed more sad than judgmental. Sadie was the first to turn away.

"Daed," Lydia said, dropping Sadie's hand and throwing her arms around her father's waist. "I thought you weren't coming in until supper time."

Vernon looked down at the girl and his face softened. "Just came back for a drink of water. My jug was empty."

"Can you stay?"

"Nee." He patted her on the head, then motioned to Sadie to take the girl's hand back.

Sadie saw the disappointment on Lydia's face as she eased the girl away from her father.

"I have to go," he said and began to turn away.

"Wait," Sadie asked. "You said no one else will work here. Why not?"

Vernon stopped and his expression shifted as he turned his attention back to Sadie. Bishop Amos had mentioned that Vernon was thirty-three, but his demeanor made him seem even older. He carried a casual air of authority like one of the church elders.

"Why do you think?" he asked in a flat tone.

"Uh, I, uh, don't know…" Sadie had no idea how to answer such a delicate question, especially while under the scrutiny of that hard stare.

"You'll find out soon enough," Vernon answered quietly.

Sadie forced a smile. "I'm sure it will be *oll recht.*" She squeezed Lydia's hand. "It's been great getting to meet Lydia." The little girl squeezed back and grinned.

"Ya. Our Lydia is a *gut maedel.*" Vernon's eyes lingered on the little girl for moment as a wistful expression passed over her face, then he frowned, jerked his attention away from Lydia and nodded toward the farmhouse. "Time to get dinner on, ain't so?"

"Oh. *Oll recht*…" Sadie stood still for a moment. "Are you going to show me around the kitchen?"

"Don't you know how to cook?"

"*Ya*. Of course."

"Then you don't need my help."

"*Nee*. I didn't mean…" Sadie cleared her throat. She usually felt at ease around people, but Vernon brought all her secret insecurities to the surface. "I just thought you might want to show me where everything is."

"Lydia can help you with that."

"*Ya*," Lydia piped up. "I'm a big girl."

"I'll see you at dinner," Vernon said, then turned away and strode back toward the yellow-green field bordering the barn. Sadie studied his broad shoulders and clenched jaw as he retreated. She felt an unexpected tug on her heart. There was so much pain in this family, simmering just beneath the surface. What had gone wrong? And more importantly, what could she do to help them?

Chapter Two

The farmhouse kitchen was well stocked, but the pale green walls were in need of a fresh coat of paint. A long butcher-block counter ran along the wall and a battered wooden table with mismatched wooden chairs stood in the middle of the worn hardwood floor. The only decor in the Plain room was a clock and a wall calendar with a nature scene. Big windows over a farmhouse sink let in the afternoon sun and gave a clear view of the farmyard, fields and rolling hills beyond the house. Sadie could see a wagon and a lone figure with a pitchfork in a distant pasture. She stared at the silhouette for a moment, trying to shake the inexplicable curiosity she felt toward Vernon Kauffman.

Sadie pulled her attention away from Vernon to rifle through the pantry and gas-powered refrigerator until she found enough ingredients to create a meal. "What do you think about roasted chicken with carrots, onions and potatoes?" Sadie asked Lydia.

"Sounds *gut* except for the onions," Lydia said as she made a face. "I don't like onions."

"We'll just use a little bit then." Sadie stacked the root vegetables from the big wooden bin into her apron and carried them across the kitchen. She let down her apron above the big sink, dropping the vegetables in with a loud thump. "And we can whip up some buttermilk biscuits too. Sound *gut*?"

"Ya!" Lydia clapped her hands once, then ran to the corner of the kitchen to grab a step stool. She carried the little wooden stool back to the counter and hopped onto it. "Ready!"

The afternoon sun slid downward in the sky as Sadie peeled and chopped. Soon, long shadows stretched across the farmyard and the breeze through the open window felt cool on her skin. Lydia stood on her stool diligently, pretending to chop carrots with a cake knife that Sadie had found stuffed in the back of a drawer. The dull, plastic blade could not possibly cut the girl—or the vegetables.

"Ready for the oven!" Sadie announced just as the front door slammed in the distance and the sound of running filled the house. There was a bang, a crash and a yelp as the footsteps drew closer, then two skinny boys shot into the kitchen in a blur of unruly auburn hair, freckles and grins.

"Oh!" Sadie spun around from the counter. "Hello, there. I'm Sadie."

The two boys glanced at each other and their grins widened before they turned their attention to their new nanny. "Hello, Sadie," they said sweetly, in unison.

"It's *wunderbar* to meet you," Sadie said. She felt the tension in her shoulders relax as she studied the boys' identical gap-toothed smiles, cute upturned noses, and freckled faces flushed red with exertion. Ned and Newt might be a handful with all that extra energy, but they were clearly sweet boys.

"Ya," the boys answered, again in unison. They shared another glance, then one of them stepped forward. "I'm Ned."

"And I'm Newt," the other one echoed. "We're eight years old, almost nine."

"And I'm older," Ned added quickly.

Newt scowled. "Only by three minutes."

"Anyway, we're almost grown-ups," Ned said. "We'll be graduated from school in a few years and ready to work on the farm with *Daed.*" He smirked. "Especially me, since I'm older."

Newt elbowed Ned in the ribs.

"Hey!" Ned shouted and rubbed his side.

"*Ach*, sorry," Newt said. "That was an accident."

Sadie decided to let their little skirmish go, for now. But when she looked down and saw the trail of muddy boot prints tracked across the kitchen floor, she knew she couldn't let that go. "You *buwe* need to leave your boots by the door for now on, please. I don't want to have to mop the floors every time you *kumme* inside."

Both boys looked chagrined. "We're sorry, Sadie!" they said. "We won't ever, ever do it again." Newt clasped his hands in front of his chest and gave a look as sorrowful as an old *groossmammi* at a funeral. Sadie thought the boy was being overly dramatic, but she let it slide. As long as he obeyed her, she could put up with his theatrics.

"*Oll recht, gut.* Take off your boots and carry them out to the porch. Then you can help me mop the floors. I just need to get this chicken in the oven."

Newt leaned over and whispered in Ned's ear. Ned nodded then turned to Sadie. "Can we get a glass of milk first? We're growing *buwe*, ain't so? And *Daed* says growing *buwe* need milk."

"*Ya!*" Newt chimed in. "And doing the chores with *Daed* works up a thirst."

"You two already did all your chores?" Sadie asked. Amish boys had a lot of work to do on a farm, especially when school was out for the summer, when they spent the days working alongside their fathers. "That's very *gut* of you."

"Ya, ya," Ned said in a distracted voice. His eyes were on the chicken and vegetables sitting in the big roasting pan beside the gas oven. "Can we get that milk, please?"

"Right." Sadie wiped her hands on a red plaid dish towel and walked over to the gas-powered refrigerator.

"Hey, Lydia," Newt said as Sadie opened the refrigerator door and pushed aside a carton of orange juice to reach the milk. *"Kumme* look at this." The children murmured and moved around the kitchen as Sadie grabbed the glass milk bottle, then pulled glasses from the cabinet.

"Look at what?" Lydia asked.

Sadie turned around in time to see Lydia staring intently at Newt's closed hands. He opened them to reveal that they were empty.

"Made you look!" Newt said and laughed. Then he looked over at Ned. Ned gave a nod and both boys bounded out of the kitchen.

"Wait!" Sadie shouted after them. "What about your milk?" The boys' footsteps faded in the distance along with their voices. "And the mopping..." Sadie sighed.

Lydia shook her head, her little hands planted firmly on her hips. "That Newt is always teasing me."

Sadie suppressed a smile. "You sound very old for your age when you talk like that."

Lydia smiled. "Do I? That's *gut.* I like being grown-up. I think it's *gut* for *Daed.* He gets tired out by Newt and Ned because they never act grown-up. They give him a headache sometimes. Then he rubs his temples and says he doesn't know what to do with such *schnickelfritz."*

Sadie chuckled. "I see."

"I'll drink one glass of milk and you can have the other," Lydia said. "That way it doesn't matter that they ran off, ain't so?"

"*Ya*, except…" Sadie looked at the muddy boot prints. She wondered if she should put her foot down and force the boys to help her mop. She had plenty of experience with *kinner*, but her siblings would not dare disobey like Newt and Ned. If an adult said to help mop, that was the end of the discussion. They had been raised with a firm but loving hand, which was expected among the Amish. Disobedience simply wasn't tolerated. So Sadie had no idea how to deal with two young boys who tore through the house like a whirlwind without any regard for her instructions.

Sadie stopped fretting long enough to pop the roasting pan in the oven, then leaned against the counter and took a long, slow sip of milk as she pondered the situation. She wiped her mouth, set down the glass and pushed away from the counter. "What does your *daed* do when Newt and Ned don't follow instructions?"

"Nothing, really," Lydia said between sips of milk. "He usually doesn't even notice."

Sadie found the mop and bucket in the corner of the pantry. She would have to figure this out on her own. And if those boys weren't used to toeing the line, well… She might really have her work cut out for her.

But Ned and Newt had been so sweet and silly when they burst into the kitchen. Surely they were just energetic, that was all. "We'll get along fine," she said to herself. There was no need to worry when there was nothing to worry about.

And, as it turned out, Ned and Newt reappeared halfway through the mopping. "*Gut, buwe. Kumme* help," Sadie said as they raced down the long hallway toward her.

"Of course, Sadie!" they said in their sweetest voices, matched by their sweetest smiles. "We're here to help!"

See, Sadie thought to herself. *There was no need to worry.* "Take this." She passed the mop handle to the nearest boy. She thought it was Newt but wasn't quite sure. They did look a lot alike. "Finish up while I check on supper."

"Oh, *ya*," he said with a big, solemn nod. "You must take care of supper. We'll handle this. Don't worry about us." The boys elbowed one another and giggled just enough to make Sadie suspect she might need to worry. But she had to get the biscuits in the oven to make sure that everything would be ready before Vernon came in from the fields. This would be her chance to show him and Arleta that she would do a *gut* job working for them.

After the poor first impression she had made on Vernon, Sadie felt extra determined to prove she was an upright Amish woman who could be trusted with the care of his household. She was especially sensitive about proving this because a lot of people in Bluebird Hills viewed her artistry with suspicion. Vernon had probably already heard that she failed to meet the community's expectations. Perhaps that was why he had been critical of her.

Sadie's stomach did a little flip-flop as she thought about seeing Vernon again. She wanted to be charitable and remember that he was still in mourning for his late wife, but that comment he had made by the water pump really had stung. She had always been of the mind that, no matter what someone is going through, there was no excuse for being rude. A frown takes as much effort as a smile. Sometimes even more. Plus, a frown doesn't feel half as good.

With that reminder, Sadie flashed the twins a big smile and headed back to the kitchen to put the last touches on her first supper in the Kauffman house.

Vernon was exhausted when he dragged himself in from the fields at sunset. His back ached and a bug bite on his neck itched. He tugged off his muddy boots and tossed them on the porch beside two pairs of dirty child-sized boots, washed up quickly and hurried into the kitchen. The rich aroma of roast chicken met him at the door. It had been a while since he had a good home-cooked meal and he felt his mood lift a little.

Sadie glanced up from where she stood setting the table, Lydia clinging to her apron with one hand, the other clutching several spoons. Sadie was pretty in a wholesome, cheerful way and had the clearest, brightest eyes he had ever seen. More than that, they sparkled when she looked at him, as if she were hiding a world of thoughts and secrets behind them. They fascinated him. *She* fascinated him.

Maybe that was why he had been hard on her when he saw her beside the water pump earlier that day. He wasn't used to being captivated by a young woman and he had no idea how to react, other than to shut his feelings down the best he knew how. Obviously, it wouldn't do to be drawn in by a bright smile, blond hair, blue eyes and rosy cheeks. If he were looking for a wife—which he absolutely was not—he would seek out a woman his own age, perhaps a widow. Someone who was stern and hardened by life, same as him. Not someone full of youthful hopes and dreams. He had adjusted to life after the accident and he wasn't about to risk losing the foothold he had finally gained. Hope was an irresponsible concept that only a young woman could indulge in. When Sadie got a little older and wiser, she would surely lose that bright smile of hers and the sparkle in her eyes would dim.

"What's the matter, *Daed*?" Lydia asked in a small voice as she handed a spoon to Sadie. Sadie set the spoon in its place and glanced up at Vernon with a concerned crinkle in her brow. Vernon deflated. He hadn't meant to look so grim. He strode over to Lydia and patted her on the head. "Nothing. I was just thinking, that's all."

"About what, *Daed*?" Lydia asked with her chin tilted upward, her big, innocent eyes on his.

"You don't like roast chicken with vegetables?" Sadie asked. He picked up on the nervous quiver in her voice, which she was clearly trying to hide behind her kind smile.

"*Ach, nee.* I mean, *ya.*" He frowned and shook his head. "What I'm trying to say is, I love roasted chicken and it smells *wunderbar*. It's been an age since we've had a *gut* home-cooked meal in this house. *Danki.*"

"Our last *kinnsmaad* didn't last until supper time," Lydia said and handed Sadie the last spoon.

"Oh." Sadie set down the spoon, then smoothed her apron. "I see." Vernon saw a flicker of determination pass over her face as she turned to the counter and began to lift the chicken out of the roasting pan and onto a big wooden serving platter. Vernon stared at the platter for a moment. It had belonged to his late wife's mother and Lorna had served countless turkeys, chickens and roasts on it. She had always loved that platter.

"It's all ready. Lydia, can you call the *buwe*? They should be finishing up their chores in the barn."

Vernon jerked from the past to the present at the sound of Sadie's voice. He cleared his throat. "And fetch *Aenti* Arleta too, *ya*?"

"Sure will, *Daed*!" Lydia galloped out of the kitchen and let the screen door bang behind her. The room filled with awkward silence. Sadie rearranged the biscuits in the serving bowl, then tucked the red plaid dishtowel over them. Vernon knew she was focusing on an unnecessary task to keep from having to speak to him. He couldn't blame her.

Vernon sighed and took a step toward her. Her eyes shot

up to his. He didn't move any closer and tried to give her a smile. He hoped it didn't look like a grimace. "I, uh, should probably apologize."

Sadie looked surprised.

"I could have been nicer when I ran into you earlier today. I'm sure you meant no harm."

Sadie gave a hesitant nod.

"I ought to give you a chance and not judge you until after you fail."

Sadie stiffened. "I don't intend to fail."

"That didn't come out the way I meant it."

"Clearly."

Now it was Vernon's turn to flinch. Sadie didn't mince words. She had a sweet smile, but she was no pushover. Instead of being offended he felt a strange sense of admiration for the young woman. He knew he could be intimidating—at least that was what he had been told. Bishop Amos had warned him several times he would never remarry unless he softened his demeanor. Of course, he didn't want to remarry so he didn't care much for the advice.

"I'm sure supper will be *gut*. I'm looking forward to it. Worked up quite an appetite today."

"Gut," she responded evenly. "I hope you like it."

Vernon saw the intelligence behind her eyes and knew she caught on that he was changing the subject. He nodded and pulled out his chair at the head of the table. Sadie set the big wooden platter in front of him with a quiet thump. She looked at him, hesitated, then said. "I accept your apology."

He grunted and picked up his fork. He was hungry enough to eat a horse. "Hope those *kinner* hurry," he muttered.

As if on cue, the screen door burst open and three sets of feet clambered into the farmhouse kitchen. Other, slower footsteps followed behind as Arleta appeared in the threshold.

"Supper already?" she asked, a slightly confused look on her face. "I must have fallen asleep for longer than I thought." Her once-glossy black hair looked dull where it showed above her *kapp* and she had dark circles under her green eyes. Her skin looked too pale.

"You ought to be getting more sun," Vernon said.

"Did I *kumme* in for supper or to get a lecture?" Arleta snapped back.

Vernon's chest tightened. He had no idea how to help his sister. Everything he said, everything he did seemed to make things worse. Which made sense, he supposed, considering her condition was his fault. He didn't blame her for being resentful and defensive. "Meet our new *kinnsmaad,* Sadie Lapp.*"

"Nice to meet you." Sadie gave a bright smile that Arleta didn't return.

Instead, Arleta released a small sigh and shuffled to the chair at the foot of the table. "It isn't the way I make it," she said as she studied the roasted chicken. Then she eased open a corner of the dishtowel that covered the bowl of biscuits. She clicked her tongue. "Are these buttermilk? They're not as fluffy as mine."

Sadie stared at her and blinked a few times.

Vernon reached out and put a hand on Arleta's. "It's *oll recht.* Her cooking might be different than yours, but it'll still be *abbeditlich.*"

Arleta pulled her hand away from Vernon's and tucked it in her lap.

"You could try and cook again, ain't so?" Vernon said softly. "I'm sure Sadie would help you. I know how much you miss it."

"I don't need help," Arleta said.

Vernon's pulse throbbed in his temple. He wanted to

put his arms around his sister and hug the hurt and anger right out of her. Instead he frowned and looked down at the white tablecloth. He hadn't seen it since Lorna passed. Sadie must have found it shoved somewhere in the back of the pantry, ironed it and put it out. "I think if you just try…"

"I have tried, Vernon." Arleta's voice was steely cold. Even the twins sat silently, waiting for the tension to break.

"I know you have, Arleta," he murmured. He studied a faint stain on the tablecloth. He remembered the day Lorna had spilled cranberry sauce there. He traced the mark absently with a forefinger. "I know you have."

"Let's eat," Sadie cut in. She began to carve the chicken, releasing steam and delicious smells from beneath the brown, crispy skin.

Ned giggled and looked at Newt. Newt shoved him and smiled. *"Ya!"* Newt shouted. "We want to eat! We can't wait to taste Sadie's cooking!"

Sadie passed Vernon the first serving and he took it with a contented sigh. At least they could have a nice meal together, in spite of all the unspoken hurt. That would do them all good.

"Can I have a drumstick?" Lydia asked. She glanced at Newt and Nate, but they didn't protest. Instead, they giggled, then covered their mouths with their napkins to hide their grins.

"Of course," Sadie answered.

Vernon saw the mischievous glint in the twins' eyes as they giggled behind their napkins, but he didn't think much of it. As long as they sat and ate and the family got through the meal without too much fuss, that was enough for him. He was too exhausted to expect more. He had felt this way for months. It was a deep exhaustion, more than just physical. It filled both his bones and his emotions until he felt as though he were wading through molasses just to get through his normal activities. As hard as that was, he knew what Arleta was going through must be much worse. She had hit her head when a car skidded into the buggy and now everything was harder for her, even simple things, like following her favorite recipes.

"Aren't we going to pray, *Daed*?" Lydia asked.

"*Ya*. Of course. Let's bow our heads." He tried not to let his mind wander again during the silent prayer and remembered to thank *Gott* for all their blessings. Sometimes he got so caught up in what he had lost it was easy to forget what he still had. "Amen," he said aloud after a minute and everyone around the table raised their heads.

Newt and Ned stared at Vernon as he picked up a generous forkful of roasted chicken and popped it in his mouth. He relaxed, expecting it to be delicious. Instead his mouth burned and his tongue felt like it had been rubbed with sandpaper. He couldn't taste the chicken at all—the sting of salt was too overpowering. He almost gagged but tried not to show his shock. He didn't want to hurt poor Sadie's feelings. Clearly the girl couldn't cook, a skill that gave an important sense of worth to an Amish woman. This would be humiliating for her.

Arleta was not so generous with her reaction. "What is this? How much salt did you use?" She grimaced and shoved her plate away. "I've never tasted anything so terrible in my life."

Sadie looked confused. "I don't understand…" She shoved a quick bite of chicken in her mouth and her eyes widened. She made a little sound in the back of her throat and shifted in her seat as she forced the bite down. "I don't… I don't understand…" She shook her head.

"You used too much salt," Arleta said. "What's there to understand?"

Ned and Newt elbowed each other and exchanged glances, then erupted with laughter.

Sadie's attention shot to the boys and her eyes narrowed. She opened her mouth, then closed it again. Her eyes stayed on Newt and Ned until their laughter died down and they looked back at her.

"What is it Sadie?" Newt asked innocently.

"Don't you want to say something?" Ned asked.

"Ya," Newt added. "Aren't you going to say something?"

Both boys leaned forward expectantly.

Sadie raised her chin a fraction and looked down at them. Instead of having their usual sparkle, her blue eyes looked steely. *"Ya.* I was just going to say that I'm sorry this mistake happened. I'm sure it won't happen again."

Newt and Ned looked surprised. "That's all you have to say?" Ned asked.

"Ya. That's all." She kept her face a dignified mask and Vernon wondered what she was thinking. *"Ach,* just one more thing—have a biscuit. That's all you're getting from me for supper, *buwe."*

Vernon stifled a smile. He suspected his rowdy *sohn* had a hand in this somehow, but Sadie wasn't going to admit defeat that easily. He found himself studying her calm expression with admiration, wondering what all she had up her sleeve. There was more to her than meets the eye, that was certain sure.

Chapter Three

Sadie was mortified. She desperately wanted to shout her innocence as Vernon stared at her with that hard, impossible-to-read expression and Arleta looked smug. Of all the terrible things to have happened while she was trying to prove her worth, why did it have to be *this*?

As much as Sadie wanted to point her finger at the twins and accuse them of pouring salt in the food, she did not. Oh, she had figured out what had happened, all right. The boys had gotten her away from the serving dish by asking for milk, then Ned salted the chicken while Newt pretended to show Lydia something to distract her attention. Clever, mischievous boys. She could have laughed at their antics if they hadn't embarrassed her so badly.

But, even though she knew what they had done, she refused to give them credit for their little scheme. If she announced their guilt, they would get exactly what she suspected they wanted—attention. So she refused to play along.

"Plain biscuits are boring," Ned said as he stared at his plate. "I like to put chicken in them."

Sadie shrugged and gave him an innocent looking smile. "*Ach*, well, you'll just have to make do, I suppose."

Ned scowled and pushed the biscuit around his plate. Sadie felt a small surge of satisfaction. Perhaps Ned would learn a lesson from this. He had no one to blame but himself from missing out on a good meal.

Newt shifted in his seat and looked uncomfortable. He glanced around the table to each of the adults, but no one paid him any mind. Sadie could tell he was disappointed by the lack of reaction that his antics had received.

Sadie felt eyes on her and turned her attention to the head of the table. Vernon was studying her with those unreadable black eyes. She almost caved under his scrutiny but managed to stay firm in her decision. If he asked her directly, *Did you oversalt the food?* she would not lie, of course. But she felt it was okay to keep the details to herself, for now. Perhaps later, when they had some privacy, she could explain.

"Well," Vernon said after staring at her for a long, uncomfortable moment. He pushed his chair back and stood up. "I think I can find us something to go with those biscuits."

Ned and Newt perked up. Their heads swiveled to follow their father's movement across the kitchen, into the walk-in pantry. Both boys deflated when Vernon reappeared holding two family-sized cans of baked beans.

"We hate baked beans!" the twins shouted.

Sadie thought she detected a faint smile on Vernon's lips. "*Ach*, well, that can't be helped."

"I love baked beans!" Lydia said and bounced in her seat.

"I know you do, Lydia," Vernon said. He set the cans on the kitchen counter, pulled a can opener from a drawer and began to open the lids.

"That's not fair, *Daed*!" Newt said.

"*Ya!*" Ned added. "Why does Lydia get what she likes?"

"Sometimes life isn't fair, *buwe*. Just so happens that this is what we have in the pantry right now."

Ned and Newt folded their arms. "Then we're not eating it," Ned said.

"Suit yourself," Vernon said as he carried the open cans to the table, set them down, then doubled back to the drawer beside the sink. He came back with two metal spoons, stuck one in each can and sat back down. "I know it's a bit informal, Sadie. But I figured you've done enough already. I don't mind eating them cold from the can if you don't."

Sadie felt a rush of confusion. Had Vernon just come to her rescue? Did he suspect the twins had a hand in this? Or was he criticizing her? What had he meant by *you've done enough already*? Was he implying that she had put in a lot of effort and deserved to rest—or that she had messed things up enough for one night?

Sadie hesitated, then reached for a can of baked beans and simply said, *"Danki,"* as she scooped a big serving of cold beans onto her plate. She had no idea what else to say, so she left it at that.

"Vernon's got the right idea," Arleta murmured as she pulled apart a biscuit, then set it back onto her plate without eating it. "You can't ruin food straight from the can."

Sadie felt heat rush to her face. There was no call for Arleta to be so combative.

Vernon sighed. "That's enough, Arleta," he said gently. "We need Sadie, whether we like it or not."

Sadie felt that rush of confusion again. *Whether we like it or not…* Was he using *we* to soften his words to placate Arleta? Or did he really mean that he didn't want Sadie there either? He had not seemed very welcoming when she first arrived, so the second explanation made more sense. Sadie looked down at her plate and shrunk into herself. She felt exposed and unwanted.

"I don't need anyone," Arleta said and stood up quickly. She lost her balance and grabbed the edge of the table for support, drew a shaky breath, then marched out of the kitchen. They heard the screen door open at the end of the hallway, then slam shut again with a faint whine of rusted hinges.

"I'm sorry," Vernon said, his face hard. "Arleta isn't herself lately." He gave no further explanation, instead turning all his attention to his plate as if no one else were at his table.

The meal was strained and silent after that. Only Lydia seemed content as she hummed to herself, swung her legs beneath the table and shoveled spoonful after spoonful of cold baked beans into her mouth.

Sadie nibbled the edge of her biscuit in the awkward quiet and stared at Arleta's untouched plate. Whatever wounds this family carried, they went even deeper than she had suspected. *I've gotten myself into an impossible situation,* Gott, she said in silent prayer. The propane lantern sputtered and cast long shadows across Vernon's expressionless face. Silverware clinked loudly in the deep silence. *I don't know the first thing about how to deal with this family's problems. But I want to do whatever I can. Could you please give me the ability to help somehow? Amen.* Sadie sopped up a few stray beans with the edge of her biscuit. Hurt and resentment tugged at her heart. *And help me not to be too uncharitable toward Arleta. She's a tough one to like,* Gott, *if you'll please forgive me for saying so. But she's gotten under my skin tonight. Amen again.*

After they finished eating, Vernon stood up without speaking and walked slowly across the kitchen. His footsteps echoed in the quiet. "Oh," he said without turning around when he reached the threshold. "You *kinner* are excused from the table." His voiced sounded tired.

Sadie frowned, pulled the napkin from her lap and tossed it onto her empty plate. Vernon's children seemed like an afterthought to him. No wonder the twins pulled such a silly stunt. Those boys were desperate for their father to notice them. And Lydia clearly craved attention too. Otherwise, she wouldn't have clung to a new nanny all day. Sadie wanted to march after Vernon and demand that he say something, *anything,* to his children. What kind of family spent an entire meal in complete silence?

Sadie had spent years longing to get away from the noise in her own family's kitchen, where there was never a moment's silence between the chatter, laughter and good-natured shouting. The Lapp house could be exhausting, but it never lacked life. Now she realized just how blessed she had been to grow up in that chaotic, noisy household, where there was plenty of love and attention to go around.

The twins clamored from their seats and began to rush from the room.

"Just a minute, *buwe*," Sadie called after them in a firm voice. "You haven't cleared your plates."

They stumbled to a stop and turned around. Ned licked his lips. "And what if we don't?"

"What will you do?" Newt added. "Tell our *Daed*?"

Sadie felt shocked. What kind of Amish child would ask such a question? This type of behavior might be common among the *Englischers*, but it was practically unheard of in her culture. A thousand responses raced through her head and she quickly chose the one that she suspected would be the most effective. "*Ne*. I won't tell your *Daed*. I'll serve baked beans for supper again tomorrow."

The twins gasped and glanced at one another.

"You have until the count of three," Sadie said. She planted her hands on her hips and stared down at them.

The boys rushed to the table and grabbed their dishes in a blur of groans and scowls, dropped the plates in the sink with a clatter and raced out the door before Sadie could say another word. She heard their footsteps pound down the hall and up the stairs, until the floorboards creaked overhead.

"Well," she said and let out a long breath. "That was quite a meal."

She felt a tug on her apron and looked down to see two big brown eyes staring up at her. "Was it my fault that the chicken had too much salt? I thought I helped, but did I do something wrong?"

Sadie dropped to a crouch and wrapped Lydia in her arms. "No, sweetie, of course it wasn't your fault. You were a wonderful good helper. Sometimes accidents happen, especially when there are naughty *buwe* about." She kissed the top of Lydia's head and stood up. "Now, how would you like to help make *Aenti* Arleta a supper plate?"

"But we just ate supper." Lydia popped a thumb in her mouth and furrowed her brow.

"Not all of us," Sadie murmured as she rifled through the pantry and refrigerator to put together a cold plate of luncheon meat, sliced cheese, biscuits and canned peaches.

"*Aenti* Arleta doesn't like us to go to the *dawdi haus*," Lydia said after watching for a while. "Maybe you shouldn't go over there. She doesn't like too much noise. It hurts her head after…" Lydia looked down and traced a crack in the floor with her big toe.

Sadie gave Lydia's arm a reassuring squeeze. "*Ya*, but I have to move in with her tonight, so I've got to go." The knots in Sadie's stomach agreed with Lydia, but she would not show it. "I figure *Aenti* Arleta's got to be hungry, ain't so? Maybe bringing food will make her feel more welcoming." Even as she said the words, Sadie wasn't so sure. But how else could she try to break the ice?

"Can I come with you?" Lydia asked.

"*Nee.* It's bedtime for little girls. But you can help me finish cleaning up the kitchen first."

After they dried the last dish and wiped the butcher-block counters, Sadie flipped off the propane lamp and followed Lydia upstairs to her bedroom. The room was small and plain, but cheerful. There was a braided rag rug on the floor, a star-pattern quilt in shades of pink on the bed and a white wooden chest with a faceless Amish doll sitting on top. Four dresses hung on pegs on the wall. Sadie could hear the twins murmuring and banging through the wall to the adjacent room.

"That's a lovely quilt," Sadie said as she pulled back the covers.

"*Mamm* made it," Lydia said. She put a little finger on one of the pale pink stars. "She liked stars so I like them too. I wish..." Lydia bit her lip.

"What do you wish?" Sadie asked gently.

"That I remembered her better. She's been gone almost a year and that's a long time."

"Ya." *For a five-year-old*, Sadie thought. *But not for the grieving widower or the injured sister-in-law. For them, the accident may as well have happened yesterday. Time flows differently for* kinner. Sadie settled onto the edge of the bed beside Lydia. "But you remember the most important thing about your *mamm*."

"I do?" Lydia peered up at Sadie with big, questioning eyes.

"Of course. You remember her love. It's always right here." Sadie tapped Lydia on the chest, over her heart. "You don't have to remember any details about your *mamm* to carry that love with you for the rest of your life. Once it's planted inside you, it's there forever."

"Oh." Lydia's forehead crinkled in thought. "I like that."

"*Gut*. Now, let's get you to sleep."

Getting Lydia to bed was easy, but Sadie knew she had a challenge ahead when it came to the twins. She tiptoed out of Lydia's room with her jaw set, prepared to do battle. But when she opened the twins' door, both boys were tucked in bed, snug as two little bugs in a rug.

"You're already in bed," Sadie said, stopping short in the doorway.

"*Ya*, of course we are," Ned and Newt said in unison with smug smiles. Sadie wondered if they were trying to impress her. Well, they were welcome to. It certainly made her life easier. "I really appreciate that, *buwe*. But did you brush your teeth and wash your faces?"

"*Ya*, we sure did," Ned said.

"Uh-huh," Newt added, still smiling.

"That's *wunderbar. Danki.* Would you like a bedtime story before I go?"

The boys' smiles dropped into scowls. "A bedtime story? We're too old for that!" Newt said.

"Yuck!" Ned shouted.

"Ach, oll recht." Sadie put up her hands in surrender and backed out of the room. "Just thought I'd ask." She stopped in the doorway. "Make sure to say your prayers. I'll wait here while you do." Sadie watched as the boys squeezed their eyes shut. Their lips moved as they prayed silently. Then Ned's eyes flew open. "Can somebody ask *Gott* for forgiveness in advance?"

"What do you mean, in advance?"

Ned shifted beneath his quilt. He gave a quick glance to Newt, who shook his head. "Um, let's say, theoretically of course, that a person did something bad that hasn't been discovered yet. Could that person go ahead and ask forgiveness before they get found out?"

Sadie's spine tingled. She was pretty sure this "something bad" was going to involve her. "Well, you ought to stop that bad thing from happening if it hasn't happened yet."

"Mmm." Ned grinned and gave an innocent shrug. "You mean *a person* should stop it, *theoretically*." He emphasized the words person and theoretically.

Sadie sighed. "*Ya*. Theoretically."

Ned shrugged again and his grin grew from innocent to downright mischievous. "And what if it's too late to stop it? Theoretically."

Sadie leaned her hip against the doorway. She could feel a headache coming on. All she wanted was to fall into a warm, snug bed and get a good night's sleep before she had to face tomorrow. "*Gott* is always ready to forgive—if a person is sorry." She gave Ned a good, hard stare. "Are you sorry?"

"Me?" Ned looked quickly from side to side, as if he were in a lineup of suspects. "I never said anything about me. What makes you think I've got anything to be sorry for?"

The base of Sadie's head began to throb. She reminded herself to stop tensing her neck. "Let's finish talking about this for tonight. It's late, ain't so?"

"*Ya*, you really should get to bed," Newt said.

Sadie narrowed her eyes. "I hope you boys aren't planning to get out of bed as soon as I turn my back."

"Us?" Newt placed a hand on his chest and looked shocked. "How could you think such a thing?"

"Well, it'll be baked beans for breakfast if you do!" Sadie said, then turned and closed the door behind her before anyone could say another word.

Sadie retrieved the aluminum-foil-covered plate from the propane-powered refrigerator, picked up the suitcase she had left by the back door and headed out to the *dawdi haus*. The night sounds of trilling insects and chirping tree frogs met her in the hot, humid summer air. A rectangle of long, yellow light fell across the bare farmyard. She looked up and saw the flickering of a propane lamp in an upstairs window. A tall silhouette came into view, blocking some of the light and casting a long shadow across the earth below. She could make out Vernon's face through the window as he stared into the distance. She sensed the longing in his gaze and felt a strange need to take his face in her hands and tell him that everything would be all right, that he wasn't alone.

But he *was* alone. Sadie just wished she could make him see that he didn't have to be. He was so busy grieving what was gone that he couldn't see what he still had left.

Vernon's dark eyes turned and looked down, directly into hers. Sadie jumped and averted her gaze. Her heart jolted into her throat and her toes tingled. She wasn't sure if it was because he caught her staring, or because his gaze did something to her that she didn't understand. She hurried away from beneath his window, cheeks burning with embarrassment, hoping that he didn't say anything the next day. She hadn't meant to watch him! And she definitely hadn't meant to get *caught* watching him.

Sadie took a deep breath before knocking on the door to the *dawdi haus*. The structure looked like a smaller version of the farmhouse with its peeling paint, tin roof and overgrown hedges. A small porch with two white rockers and a trellis of rose vines could have been inviting, if the vines had been tended. But the dead, brown plant gave an air of sadness to what must have once been a quaint and cozy home.

"Go away, please!" someone shouted from behind the door.

"Oh." Sadie hesitated. "It's me."

"*Ya.* I know. Who else would it be?"

Sadie knocked again. "I brought you something to eat."

There was silence on the other side of the door. Sadie stood and waited. She was just about to give up when a lock clicked and the doorknob slowly turned. "It's nothing special," Sadie added as the door cracked open. "Just what I could find to throw together for you." The door blocked most of Arleta's face, but Sadie could see she had traded her white *kapp* for a blue kerchief knotted at the nape of her neck. The room behind her was dim and smelled faintly of old books and wood smoke.

"You didn't have to do that," Arleta said. Her brow furrowed. "Why *would* you do that?"

Sadie's brow crinkled in confusion, just like Arleta's. "Why wouldn't I?"

Arleta didn't answer. Instead, she opened the door wide enough to reach for the plate. *"Danki,"* she said as she pulled it inside. Then the door closed with a quiet bang and Sadie was left standing there, staring at the weathered paint. She sighed and knocked again. "Could you please let me in? I'm staying here, ain't so?" Sadie began to wonder if she'd misunderstood. But where else would she sleep?

The door slowly cracked open, then Sadie heard the sound of footsteps retreating. "I'd forgotten," Arleta said. Her voice came from some distance away. "Sometimes I forget things."

"Oh." Sadie pushed the door open the rest of the way. "That's *oll recht.*" She saw Arleta across the small living room. Sadie could also make out a glider chair, a sofa and a quilt rack in the dim light. A cast-iron stove stood in the corner, unused during the warm summer months.

"*Nee*, it's not," Arleta said as she settled into the glider.

"I'm the strange old maid who can't remember anything, ain't so?" She balanced the plate on her lap and peeled off the aluminum foil.

"*Nee*. I don't think so."

Arleta sighed. "Think what you like. It's true all the same."

There were so many things that Sadie wanted to say to Arleta, but she was afraid none of them would sound right. There was too much loss here to be addressed with a few trite sentences. "I guess I'll go on to bed," she said instead. "*Danki* for having me."

Arleta's face clouded. "It wasn't my choice." She nodded toward a doorway. "That's your room."

Still at a loss for words, Sadie walked away without speaking, her suitcase gripped tightly in her hand.

Her new room was small and sparsely furnished, but tidy. The walls had been whitewashed a long time ago and now had a weathered, rustic feel. An old-fashioned wrought iron bedframe held a narrow mattress. A stand with a white porcelain washbasin and towel sat beneath a small window. There was no other furniture, just a few wooden pegs on the wall to hang her clothes and a wooden crate that served as a bedside table. The words Fresh Peaches were still faintly visible on the wooden slats. A kerosene lantern and book of matches sat on top.

Sadie quickly lit the kerosene lantern before shutting the door behind her and taking a deep breath. The light from the lantern cast a warm, familiar glow through the cozy space. The room wasn't much, but it was all hers. Sadie had never had a room to herself before and she felt suddenly more grown-up than she ever had in her twenty-two years of life. No one's snores or cold feet would wake her up tonight, that was certain sure.

She opened the window to cool the room with night air,

then changed into a crisp, white cotton nightgown, washed her face and brushed her teeth in the basin and pulled back the covers with a happy smile. She was safe, warm and snug. Until a dark shadow twisted across the sheet. Sadie's heart plummeted to her feet as her eyes registered what she was seeing. A snake. A big, long, ferocious snake. In her bed!

Sadie let out a scream loud enough to shake the walls of the little cottage. An instant later the door flew open and Arleta rushed into the room as the door banged against the wall.

"What's happened?" Arleta shouted.

"Snake!" Sadie said as she flattened herself against the beadboard paneling, as far from the bed as she could get. "I don't like snakes. I really don't like snakes!"

Arleta's eyes narrowed and she eased toward the bed.

"No!" Sadie shrieked. "It isn't safe."

Arleta took another determined step forward.

Sadie pressed herself against the wall so hard she could feel the rough wood digging into her skin. "You shouldn't…"

"Mmm. We'll see about this." Arleta's face took on a calm, knowing look. She glanced at Sadie, then back at the bed, grabbed a corner of the covers and threw them all the way back. The long green snake lay coiled and still, fully exposed on the bare sheet. Arleta stared for a moment, then leaned over and grabbed it.

Sadie gasped. "What are you doing?"

Arleta cracked a smile—the first one Sadie had seen from her. "There's nothing to be scared of." She looked directly in Sadie's eyes, grinned and tossed the snake to her. Sadie screamed, but instinctively caught it before it hit her chest. Her fingers sank into…rubber. "Wait." It took a few beats for Sadie to realize what was happening. "This isn't real!"

Arleta's smile widened. "*Nee*. It's a toy."

"But…" Sadie stood in awkward silence, the toy snake dangling from her hand.

Arleta began to laugh. It was a good, genuine belly laugh, the kind that can't be resisted. Sadie felt all her fear evaporate. "What was I thinking?" she asked before the laughter overtook her too. Knees weak from relief, she slid down the wall, landed hard on her bottom and kept laughing.

Arleta dropped onto the bed, holding her belly and wiping her eyes. "Those naughty *kinner*!" Arleta managed to get out between gasps for breath. "You should have seen your face!"

"You were just as bad!" Sadie said. "You threw it at me." She gulped for air, her belly aching. "You scared me worse than they did."

"*Ach!* I told you it wasn't real first."

"Did you? I don't think you did."

Arleta looked sheepish. "*Nee?* Sorry. Didn't mean to scare you…much."

"Arleta! You weren't in on this were you?"

"*Nee*, of course not. But I know what those *buwe* are capable of."

"I can't remember the last time I was so scared!" Sadie said as another wave of laughter overtook her. "How *lecherich* of me!*"

"*Ya*, it was ridiculous for certain sure!" Arleta agreed.

But it had been worth it. Sadie had not dreamed that she and Arleta could share such a genuine, spontaneous moment together. The tension between them had lifted, if only for a moment.

The front door slammed open, footsteps pounded through the living room and Vernon stormed into the bedroom. "What's happened?" he shouted. His tall frame seemed too big for the small room. "Sadie? What's wrong? Have you fallen?" He rushed to her and dropped to the floor. His large, calloused hands gripped her arms gently but firmly. Sadie tried to swallow her laughter to answer him. He stared into her eyes, face hard, then turned to Arleta, his hands still holding Sadie steady. "Has she lost her senses?"

Arleta pushed herself up from where she had been lying on the bed, collapsed with laughter.

"And you?" Vernon added in a rush. "Have you fallen too? What's going on?"

"We're fine," Arleta said. The smile died on her face and she slipped back into her usual, serious self. She brushed off the front of her dress and smoothed her apron. "Just fine."

"*Nee*, I heard screaming and then… I don't know…crying?"

He turned his attention back to Sadie and studied her face, his brow furrowed. "Tears," he said and lifted a finger to gently wipe the moisture from Sadie's reddened cheek. "What's made you cry? Are you hurt?" His dark eyes bore into hers, fiery with concern.

"*Ach, nee.*" Sadie shook her head. The laughter had completely vanished and now her body felt frozen, unsure how to react to the turn of events. Had Vernon just touched her face with the softest, most caring touch she could have imagined?

"Then what's happened?"

"I'm *oll recht*. It was a mistake. We were laughing."

"Laughing?" A look of mortification crossed over Vernon's face, then his expression hardened, his hand fell from her arm and he jerked back from her. "I'm sorry. I didn't mean to… I shouldn't have…" He cleared his throat. "I thought something was wrong. I thought you needed me. Not me. Help. I thought you needed help."

"It's okay," Sadie said in a soft voice. She looked down,

unable to meet his eyes after that unexpected touch. "It was an easy mistake. I found a snake in my—"

"A snake?" Vernon tensed. "I'll take care of it. Don't worry." His face took on a no-nonsense look. "You two get out of here fast and let me handle it."

"Nee." A smile tugged at Sadie's lips. She looked back up at him. "It was just a toy snake. The *buwe* must have put it in my bed. That's why I screamed. But then when we realized what had happened, it just seemed so funny because I had been so afraid over nothing. And then when Arleta threw it at me…" She shook her head, unable to keep her smile from growing into a grin. "I can't explain why it was so funny. It just was."

"Can't remember the last time I've laughed so hard," Arleta said from where she sat on the bed. "Those *buwe* fooled her *gut.*"

"But not you?"

"Nee."

Vernon raised an eyebrow.

"Oll recht. Maybe a little. But only for a minute."

Vernon turned back to Sadie. "You sure you're okay?" His eyes still held concern, but now they showed distance too. Sadie could sense he was pulling back from her. Of course he would, after embarrassing himself by wiping the tear from her cheek. She still felt rattled by that display of kindness.

And she felt even more rattled by the warmth she felt deep in her chest from that touch.

Who was the man behind the mask that Vernon Kauffman wore?

Chapter Four

Vernon woke up before the rooster crowed the next morning. The sun rose early this time of year, but at this hour the world was still painted a deep black. He sighed and fumbled for the matchbook on the bedside table. The room flared with light when he struck the match, and he caught his reflection in the window. He thought he looked old and tired and wished he could go back to sleep. Instead, he lit the kerosene lantern and pushed himself out from beneath the warm, nine-patch calico quilt that Lorna had made when they first married. The worn floorboards felt cool beneath his bare feet.

He strained to hear any noise from the floor beneath him. There was only silence. He exhaled and hurried across the room to where his work clothes hung from a row of pegs on the wall. The last thing he wanted to do was see Sadie in the kitchen this morning. He had gotten up early enough that, if he dressed quickly, he should be able to avoid her.

His eyes cut toward the *dawdi haus* outside the window, but he could only make out the shine of his kerosene light against the glass. Surely Sadie and Arleta were still asleep. He shrugged into his plain blue work shirt then pulled on a pair of black trousers so fast that he lost his balance, hopped in place twice and bumped the wall with his shoulder before righting himself. Vernon grimaced. He shouldn't be running from Sadie as if he were a scared little boy fleeing a big bad wolf.

Even so, he didn't slow his escape. He clicked off the kerosene lantern, then hit the stairs running, took them two at a time, grabbed the handrail and propelled himself around the stairwell's tight corner and into the living room like a slingshot.

And thudded directly into Sadie Lapp.

Her eyes widened and her mouth flew open, but no noise came out as she bounced back from him. Vernon's hands shot forward before she could fall, clutched her upper arms firmly and set her back on her feet. He kept his grip on her, worried that she might not be steady yet. Their eyes met and he knew his expression must mirror the shock on her face. He realized that he was still holding her and yanked his hands away as if he had touched a hot stove.

"I'm sorry," he said as he backed up a step. Everything in him wanted to run away or just sink into the floor and disappear. Forever. He had done everything he could to avoid Sadie but had run right into her. Literally. "I uh, I don't know what happened."

Sadie's blue eyes crinkled at the corners as she laughed. "You ran into me."

"*Ya*. I can see that. I meant…" He stared at her as he tried to explain.

Sadie's smile faded and she looked down.

Vernon realized he was scowling at her.

"Is something wrong?" she asked, her voice more serious this time. "You came down those stairs awful fast."

"*Nee*. Just wanted to get a *gut* start on the day. A lot of work to do on the farm this time of year."

"You don't want breakfast first?"

"I, uh, I don't need anything…not right now…" Vernon felt so flustered by Sadie's clear blue eyes and kind expression that he couldn't think straight. All he knew was that he had to get out of there as quick as he could. "I've got to get to the fields," he muttered as he stormed past her.

"But it's too dark to see."

He could feel Sadie's eyes on his back. His neck tingled and his face felt hot.

"That's what lanterns are for."

"You don't have one."

Vernon looked down at his hands and skidded to a stop. "Uh, *nee*, I…" He shook his head to clear his thoughts. "There's one in the barn," he said, then raced out the door, letting the screen slam behind him.

The air was still cool this time of morning and he shivered as he jogged across the farmyard. His foot caught on something in the dark and he stumbled, muttered to himself and continued toward the barn. He needed to clear the farmyard but couldn't face that job yet. He reminded himself that was a problem for another time. He wouldn't think about it right now. Instead, it would remain one more burden that weighed on him each day, like an invisible yoke around his shoulders.

Vernon pushed open the big barn door. The wood creaked as the familiar, earthy smells of animals and hay billowed toward him. His draft horse, Big Red, whinnied in the dark and stomped a heavy hoof. Vernon felt along the rough wooden wall until his hand hit the kerosene lamp hanging from a nail. He reached for the matches he kept on a shelf beside it and cringed. There were none left and he hadn't brought any with him. Now he would have to go back to the house and face Sadie. Or he could sit in the dark and wait for the sun. That felt like the better option, as ridiculous as it was for a grown man to hide in his barn from a sweet, twenty-two-year-old woman who wouldn't hurt a fly.

But after he had wiped the tears from her cheek last night, he couldn't possibly face her. How could he have misread that situation so badly? All he knew was that his heart had rocketed into his throat and his body had broken into a sweat when he had heard her scream. Everything after that had been instinct.

Until he had regained his senses and realized he had made a fool of himself. Then he had had no idea of what to do. Maybe another man would have joined in Sadie's and Arleta's laughter. He wished he could have found a way to laugh the entire situation away. But all he had been able to think about was how Sadie's tears had felt on his fingertips and how she had looked up at him, for the briefest instant, as if he really had been a hero.

Maybe he had imagined that last part. But what if he hadn't? Vernon slid down the wall and settled into a comfortable position on the dusty barn floor to wait for daylight. It was too dangerous to venture back into the farmhouse. He was no hero and he had to make certain sure Sadie understood that, no matter what.

Sadie was still feeling dazed from her run-in with Vernon when she heard the jangle of a harness and the rhythmic clip-clop of a horse's hooves on the dirt driveway. She set down the glass she had been using to cut out biscuits and wiped the flour from her hands with a blue checkered dishcloth. Before she finished straightening her *kapp*, the back door flew open and an elderly woman strode into the kitchen. Her body language seemed too quick and determined for her advanced age.

"Viola," Sadie said in a flat voice. "How lovely to see you."

Viola raised an eyebrow. "You ought not tell lies, you know."

"*Ach*, well…"

Viola Esch gave a dismissive wave as she sailed past Sadie. "I'm not here to be liked. I'm here to help. That's my job, ain't so?"

Sadie watched Viola settle into one of the mismatched kitchen chairs. The elderly woman propped her cane against the table and sighed. "Now, that sure feels good to sit down. I'll have a cup of *kaffi*. Cream, no sugar. Young people like their drinks too sweet, these days. Rots the brain, if you ask me. Not to mention the teeth. I've still got a few of my own, you know."

Sadie blinked a few times. "*Kaffi*. Right." She let out a long breath of air and started for the woodstove. "Coming right up."

"Make it three cups."

Sadie spun back around. "That's a lot of *kaffi*."

"It's not all for me, silly goose. The bishop and his wife are here too."

Sadie stifled a smile. Of course Viola would have weaseled her way into the bishop's visit. She had a special talent for knowing everything that was happening in Bluebird Hills—and sharing her opinion about it.

There was a soft knock on the door frame, then Edna, the bishop's wife, appeared behind the screen. She was plump and had cheerful red cheeks and gray hair tucked beneath her neatly starched *kapp*. "Hello, there," she said, waiting until she was invited to come inside.

Sadie glanced at Viola with a pointed look before smiling

at Edna and motioning for her to come in. "*Willkumme.* I was just making *kaffi* for the four of us. Cream and sugar?"

"*Ya,*" Eda said as she wiped her black athletic shoes on the doormat. "And make enough for five. Amos has gone to fetch Vernon."

"Oh. *Oll recht.*" Sadie's stomach did a little jump into her chest. She swallowed down the feeling and turned to the woodstove. The memory of his fingertips on her cheek the night before flashed through her. Sadie didn't understand her reaction to that moment—and she didn't want to. Vernon Kauffman was stern and reclusive. He was not the sort of man to stir up any kind of warmth in her heart. He was not a hero, even though he had made her feel that way last night. That was too confusing. It did not fit his character.

Or did it?

"He's already out working," Sadie said. "Maybe we ought to let him stay on task." Sadie checked the pot of water she had put on to boil before Viola and Edna had arrived. She had not slept well the night before and had already planned to make a big jug of coffee for herself. The water was at a roiling boil, so Sadie walked to the counter and began opening and closing cabinets, searching for supplies.

"Second to the left, top shelf," Viola said.

Sadie smiled. Leave it to Viola to know the contents of every cabinet in Bluebird Hills.

Edna appeared at Sadie's side and began to pull a set of white coffee mugs from a row of hooks on the wall above the counter. "How are you, Sadie?"

"*Ach*, I'm fine. I'm great." Sadie stood on her tiptoes to reach a battered metal tin on the top shelf of the second-to-left cabinet. The words Ground Coffee were written in black crayon on a piece of masking tape on the side of the tin.

Edna hesitated. "Really, Sadie. How are you?" She studied a chip in one of the white mugs as she set it on the counter. "This may not be an easy adjustment for you. This home…" she frowned as she searched for words "…has known more than its share of sorrow."

Sadie wasn't sure how to answer that. "I just want to help," she said as she pulled a glass jug and a box of paper filters from the cabinet and set them beside the coffee grounds. "But I don't know how."

The back door swung open and the bishop swept in with a big grin and a loud "Hello!" He popped off his straw hat, exposing a bald head with a few strands of unruly gray hair.

"Your hair, dear," Edna said.

"Ach." Amos grinned, shrugged his shoulders and smoothed a wrinkled hand across his bare head, missing the strands of hair that were sticking up. He winked at Sadie. "At least I've got some left, right, Edna?"

Edna shook her head but smiled fondly at her husband.

"The *kaffi* isn't quite ready," Sadie said. "Just give me a minute."

Amos hung his straw hat on a peg by the door, then settled into one of the mismatched kitchen chairs. "That's just fine. We came a bit early for visitors. But we wanted to see how you were getting on."

Before Sadie could answer, a shadow fell across the doorway and Vernon appeared behind the screen, his large frame taking up the entire space. Sadie closed her mouth and turned toward the counter. She busied herself by dampening a filter, securing it over the top of the jug, then scooping several spoonfuls of ground coffee beans into the filter. She forced herself not to look at Vernon as she walked to the stove to grab the pot of boiling water. Sadie wondered if it would be worse to see a frown of disapproval on his face or that look of care and concern from last night. Either one would leave her confused.

Sadie heard the slow scrape of a chair behind her and knew that Vernon was sitting down at the table. His heavy boots shuffled against the hardwood floor as he made himself comfortable. Sadie kept her back to him as she poured the boiling water over the coffee grounds in the paper filter. She stared at the *kaffi* that began to drip into the jar below.

"*Kumme* join us while that brews," Edna said.

Sadie bit her lip and turned to the small group. Edna patted the chair beside her. "You don't seem yourself today."

"Where's that cheerful smile you're so famous for?" Amos asked.

Sadie blushed. "*Ach*, I don't know about that."

"No one has a smile as big as yours, Sadie," Edna said. "But Amos is right. We've barely seen it today." Her eyes moved to Vernon, then back to Sadie. "Are you *oll recht*?"

"Of course I am," Sadie answered cheerfully as she forced a huge grin. Amos and Edna exchanged a knowing glance and Sadie knew she hadn't fooled them. Vernon's gaze was on his hands, which were folded on the table in front of him. He didn't look any happier to be there than Sadie did.

"She shouldn't have come," he said without looking up.

The sparkle left Amos's eyes as he cut them toward Vernon. "I think you better explain," Amos said. "Otherwise, Sadie might not feel welcome here, ain't so?"

"It's my *buwe*. They aren't easy to manage."

"They mean well," Sadie said.

Vernon raised his eyebrows, but said nothing.

"And Lydia, she's a *wunderbar maedel*. She just needs a little—" Sadie cut herself off. Now was not the time to criticize Vernon's parenting. "I'll check the *kaffi*." Sadie stood up so fast she nearly toppled her chair. Viola's discerning gaze followed her all the way to the counter.

"Hmm." Amos ran his fingers through his long gray beard. "So the problem is just your *buwe*?"

Vernon shifted in his seat. "Sadie's a *gut* worker so far. I have no complaints."

Sadie stiffened as she walked to the counter. It wasn't exactly the highest praise.

"No complaints…" Amos put up his hands. *"Oll recht."* His eyes held a quiet wisdom that Sadie had seen in them many times before. He always seemed to know what others didn't pick up on. Maybe he and Viola were alike in that regard— just not in the way they communicated it. As if on cue, Viola piped up from her place at the table. "We can all see you're too hard on the poor girl, Vernon. Would a smile or a kind word kill you?"

"Ach. It's not like that." But the look on Vernon's face showed he knew that was exactly what it was like.

Viola leaned over the table, toward Vernon. "And while you're at it, how about taking your family out for once. You've got Sadie to help watch the *kinner* while you're out visiting, so you don't have an excuse anymore. She'll help keep those rowdy *buwe* in line." Viola turned her attention to Sadie. "Won't you, Sadie?"

Sadie fumbled and nearly spilled the brewed *kaffi* as she poured it from the jar into the row of white mugs on the counter. "I can…try…"

Viola snorted. "You're more capable than you give yourself credit for." She tapped her cane on the hardwood floor for emphasis. "You always have been. Even if you do spend too much of your time and effort putting squiggles on canvas."

"You mean my paintings?"

"*Ya*. That's what I said."

Sadie wanted to respond, *Not exactly*, but managed to keep her thoughts to herself.

"*Danki* for coming," Vernon said as he abruptly stood up from the table. "But I really have to get to work. Got to get the last of the sweet corn planted."

Vernon zipped out of the room so quickly that he practically left a trail of smoke behind him. Sadie felt her cheeks heat up and kept her eyes on her coffee. It must be obvious to everyone that Vernon was avoiding her. They would all think that he must really dislike her to have run out on the bishop like that. Sadie heard the door open and close with a bang but didn't look up. She hoped no one would mention what had just happened.

"Well, he couldn't get out of here fast enough," Viola muttered.

Sadie sighed. Viola wasn't going to let it go. "I'm sorry, Bishop Amos," Sadie said. She wrapped her fingers around the warmth of the coffee mug as she tried to find the words. "Vernon doesn't like me very much. I'm afraid this wasn't such a *gut* idea." She shook her head. "I've not done a *gut* enough job with the *buwe* and—"

Viola hit the bottom of her cane against the floor and Sadie jumped at the sudden noise. "Nonsense," Viola said. "You're not the problem. Vernon is."

Edna reached over and gave Viola a gentle pat on the arm to silence her. "I think what Viola is trying to say is, well, Vernon hasn't been himself since the buggy accident. He has gotten used to being alone and doesn't know how to welcome someone into his home."

Viola snorted. "I wasn't *trying* to say anything. I said exactly what I meant to say. *Ya*, Vernon's been through a terrible loss, but that doesn't change the fact that he's the problem—even if what happened is not his fault."

Edna gave a thoughtful nod, then glanced at her husband.

"Vernon's got a *gut* heart," Bishop Amos said.

"I'd be the first to tell somebody that," Viola said.

"*Ya*, you're usually the first to tell anything," Edna said.

"I'm going to take that as a compliment," Viola muttered.

Edna smiled sweetly, as if it had been meant as one, and Sadie bit her lip to keep from chuckling.

Amos raised an eyebrow at his wife but couldn't hide the twinkle in his eye.

Sadie took a sip of coffee and then, when no one else spoke, she said what was on her mind. "I'm sorry, but I think this has been a mistake. I want to stay and do something to help, but…" She wasn't sure how to end that sentence. The thought of Lydia's sweet little hand clinging to hers tugged at her heart. And then there were the twins—as mischievous as they were, she knew they were acting out for a reason. And Arleta. Well, she needed nothing short of a miracle, and Sadie wanted to be a part of bringing that, even though it seemed impossible. Vernon's ever-present scowl reminded her just how impossible every time she saw him.

"Vernon wants you here." Amos's voice pulled Sadie from her thoughts.

"*Danki* for saying so, but…" She tried to think of a polite way to say what she knew to be true. It wouldn't do to contradict the bishop.

"There is no 'but,'" Viola said. "*Youngies* today." She raised her eyes toward the heavens as though she were undergoing a great trial. "Can you not see what's right in front of your eyes?"

"That Vernon wants to be left alone?" Sadie asked in a halting voice.

"*Ach*, Sadie, *Gott* gave you more sense than that. Can't you see how flustered Vernon is around you?"

"*Ya*. Of course. That's my point."

"And why do you think he's so flustered by you?"

"Because I'm invading his private space. He's a man who likes to keep to himself. He doesn't want to be bothered."

"Are you sure about that?" Viola asked as she gave Sadie a pointed look.

"Are you implying—" Sadie cut off her sentence and shook her head so hard that the strings of her *kapp* bounced against her cheeks. "You don't mean…" Sadie didn't want to say it out loud, in case she had misunderstood. Surely Viola wasn't implying that Vernon Kauffman might have feelings for her?

Amos held up his hands, palms outward. "Let's not put the cart before the horse. But I do think it's a *gut* thing you're here. *Gott* works in mysterious ways. Let's see how He might use you to help this family. You have a way with people, ain't so?"

"I want to help, I really do," Sadie said. "But I feel like they don't want me here. Well, except for little Lydia." She smiled at the memory of cooking dinner side by side the night before.

"Give it time," Edna said.

"You're free to leave with us, of course," Amos said. "But Edna's right. You might be surprised at what *Gott* can do, if you let Him."

Sadie remembered all the hard stares and unwelcoming comments she had endured in less than twenty-four hours. Could she really stay where she wasn't wanted?

"You know, sometimes people don't know what they really want," Amos said, as if reading her thoughts.

"Or they don't know how to communicate what they really want, even if they do know," Edna added.

"Vernon wants her here," Viola said. She used her cane to push herself up from her chair, signaling that the conversation was over. "It's clear as day. That's all that needs to be said."

Sadie wasn't sure she agreed. But she knew there was no point in arguing her case. And besides, what if they were right? The thought sent a tiny thrill up her spine that she didn't want to feel. A surge of embarrassment quickly followed. How could she feel *anything* for Vernon Kauffman? Of all the men in Bluebird Hills, he was the last one who would have feelings for her. And, if she knew what was good for her, she ought to have none for him. Anything else was downright ludicrous. And perhaps, even dangerous. Hearts were fragile things, and Vernon did not seem like the kind of man who would tread gently when it came to matters of the heart.

Chapter Five

Sadie barely had time to clear the table after the visitors left before the twins barreled into the kitchen.

"How did you sleep last night, Sadie?" Ned asked as he skidded to a stop bedside her.

Newt rocked onto his tiptoes and down again, overflowing with excited energy. "*Ya!* Did you sleep well?"

Sadie finished drying the last coffee mug in the sink, then turned around. "Like a baby."

Ned and Newt glanced at one another, then back at her.

"But—" Newt started, but Ned elbowed him in the ribs.

"*Ach*, I just couldn't keep my eyes open. The *dawdi haus* is nice and cozy, *ya*?"

"Nothing kept you from sleeping?" Newt pushed. "Nothing at all?"

"*Nee.* Nothing at all." Sadie suppressed a smile. "Oh, unless you mean that cute little snake who came to say goodnight."

"Cute!" Ned and Newt shouted in unison.

"*Ya.*"

"But nannies can't think snakes are cute!" Ned bellowed. "Why not?"

"They just can't!" Ned said. "It's against the rules."

"Hmm, well. I guess this nanny breaks the rules."

"But…" Ned's mouth gapped open. Newt shook his head. "Nannies hate snakes!"

Sadie lifted her shoulders in an exaggerated shrug and raised her hands, palms up. "Not this one. Guess I'm just different."

"But now what do we do to—" Newt elbowed Ned to stop the sentence short. He gave Ned an almost imperceptible shake of the head, then cleared his throat and saddled up to Sadie. "Well, what do you hate? Mice? Snails? Slugs? There's got to be something."

"Mmm. Good question." Sadie tapped her finger against her lips as if she were deep in thought. "Kittens probably."

"Kittens?" Ned and Newt asked with narrowed eyes.

"*Ya.* They terrify me."

The twin's eyes narrowed even more.

"And puppies. I'd hate to find one of those in my bed."

Ned gave an exaggerated sigh, then leaned into Newt, whispered something to him, and they both shook their heads. "Never mind," Ned said. The boys turned and headed toward the back door. Newt's arms were folded in frustration.

"Not so fast," Sadie said. "You've got breakfast to eat."

"We're not hungry," Ned said.

"Yeah, we're not hungry," Newt echoed.

Sadie smiled. "*Gut.* Then we can get started right away."

The twins stopped walking and turned back toward Sadie. "What do you mean?" Ned asked.

Newt looked skeptical. "Get started on what?"

"Well, since you have enough time on your hands to play tricks on the new *kinnsmaad*, then you have enough time to help me clear the yard today."

"We've got too many chores to do that!" Ned said. "We have to help *Daed* with the farm work." Sadie suspected the twins spent more time running around the farm than actually helping—and Vernon didn't seem to notice or care. Maybe he was still too engulfed by grief.

"Ya!" Newt piped up. "There's no way we can work in the yard. Get Lydia to help instead."

"She will help. We'll all going to do it together. Then I'm going to make sure you help your *Daed.*"

Lydia wandered into the kitchen, yawning and rubbing her eyes. "Did I just hear my name?"

Sadie grinned at her. "Perfect timing. I was just telling your *brudres* that you are going to be a *gut* helper today."

Lydia beamed.

"And we were telling Sadie that we have to do our regular chores before we can do anything else."

"What chores were you planning on doing?" Sadie raised an eyebrow.

"Uh…" Ned and Newt looked at each other.

"If I had to guess, I'd say you *buwe* were headed to the creek, not the barn."

Ned and Newt shook their heads.

Sadie pointed to the towel that each boy held in his hand. Ned sighed and Newt scowled.

Sadie just smiled. "Let's get started."

"You can't make us." Newt gave her a challenging stare.

"Ne, I can't. But I can serve baked beans for every meal until you do."

"You can't do that," Ned said.

"I sure can. And I will."

"Daed won't let you," Newt said.

"You sure about that?" Sadie asked.

Newt frowned and leaned into Ned. They whispered back and forth before pulling apart again. *"Oll recht,"* Ned said. "We'll help clear the yard. But not because you're making us—because you're not. We're going to help because we decided we want to."

"Ah, I see," Sadie said with a knowing smile. "That's *gut*. I bet you *buwe* are just excited to see your *Daed*'s reaction. He'll be so happy when he comes in from the fields this afternoon."

A flicker of hope passed over the boys' faces that made them seem suddenly vulnerable, for all their troublemaking. Sadie's heart melted at the sight.

"Do you really think so?" Newt asked.

"*Ya*, I do," Sadie said.

Ned's chest puffed out and he turned toward the door. "I'll get the rake out of the barn."

"And I'll get the wheelbarrow!" Newt added, racing to pass Ned. They both flew out of the kitchen in a blur of black pants, blue shirts and red freckles, followed by the slam of the screen door.

Sadie, Lydia, Ned and Newt spent the next hour clearing trash and weeds from the yard. Sadie found a broken jug, an old leather shoe and five cracked flowerpots. She shook her head and wondered how Vernon had allowed his yard to fall into such a state of disrepair. Next, Sadie turned her attention to the overgrown kitchen garden. They weeded the beds, then hauled buckets of water from the pump to water the perennials struggling to survive. Soon, her back was aching and the twins were losing steam. "I'm sick of this," Ned announced and kicked a clod of dirt. The dirt landed on Newt's knee. "Hey!" he shouted. "Did you see that, Sadie? Ned's throwing dirt on me!" Newt reached down and gathered a handful of dirt in retaliation.

"I did not!" Ned shouted. "I'm *kicking* dirt on you! And besides, it was an accident."

Sadie straightened up and stretched her back. "I wouldn't throw that dirt, if I were you, Newt," Sadie said.

"Why not?"

"Because if you do, you'll miss out on the fun."

Newt looked skeptical, but the hand clutching the dirt didn't move. "What fun?"

Sadie flashed a mischievous grin. "*This* fun." Then she picked up a bucket and sloshed the water onto Newt.

The children froze for an instant, then Newt grinned mischievously and emptied his bucket of water over Lydia's head. She sputtered and blinked, then squealed and splashed her bucket of water back at him. Ned flung his water onto both Lydia and Newt. "Let's do it again!" Lydia shouted and took off for the pump with her empty bucket. Ned and Newt charged after her. "You're next, Sadie!" Newt shouted as he raced away. Sadie barreled after him to refill her own bucket.

They all spent the next twenty minutes laughing and splashing one another, until they were too worn-out to move and collapsed on their backs in a patch of brown grass.

"Look!" Lydia said and pointed to a fluffy white cloud in the sky above. "It's a horse just like Big Red!"

Sadie smiled. "Sure is."

Ned squinted. "Looks more like a cow to me."

"Or a hippopotamus," Newt said. They all laughed.

"Well," Sadie said as she pushed herself up and brushed her hands. "Time to get back to it."

Newt groaned. "I'm tired out now." Leaves stuck to his soaking wet, auburn hair and a streak of dirt covered his chin.

"It won't take long to finish watering the vegetable beds," Sadie said. "And besides, it was worth it to have a little fun.

Sometimes taking time for fun helps you get more done in the long run."

"I don't think *Aenti* Arleta would agree with that," Lydia said.

Sadie looked toward the *dawdi haus* to see Arleta standing on the porch with both hands on her hips and a frown on her face. Sadie stood up and waved. Arleta didn't wave back. Instead, her frown deepened. Sadie felt suddenly self-conscious. She wrung the water from the skirt of her dress and straightened her *kapp*. She could feel Arleta's judgmental stare on her but refused to look at her again.

"I don't want to get back to work," Ned said. He stayed sprawled on the ground, arms and legs outstretched.

"Tell you what, let's set a goal. If we can get this *fer- hoodled* yard looking *gut* before supper time, then we all get ice cream." She paused for effect. "*With* supper."

Ned's head popped up. "With chocolate sauce?"

"Extra chocolate sauce," Sadie said.

Ned exploded from the ground. "Let's go!"

"And sprinkles!" Lydia added as she skipped toward her water bucket.

"All the sprinkles you want." Sadie bent down to pick up her own bucket. "But the best reward will be the look on your *Daed*'s face when he sees what you've done for him." A cheer erupted from the children as they redoubled their efforts.

Vernon felt hot and tired. The July sun had beaten against his back all day as he worked along the long rows of sweet corn. He pulled off his hat, wiped his forehead with a bandana, then replaced it. He had kept on task well past lunch and his stomach growled. It was time to get home and get a hearty meal before he had to do the evening chores.

Insects buzzed in the still, humid air as Vernon led Big Red back to the barn. He wondered what he would find when he reached the farmyard. He could only hope that the twins hadn't caused too much trouble and that Arleta had managed to be hospitable. Vernon knew he had already caused enough damage on his own. He grimaced as he remembered telling the bishop that Sadie should never have come to work for him. If she gave up on the family and left, he didn't know what he would do. Despite what he had said, she felt like his last hope, especially since his family had already been rejected by virtually every other woman who might be willing to work as a nanny for them.

He couldn't blame the nannies. Snakes in their beds, frogs in the kitchen sink—whatever mischief the boys could conjure—not to mention Arleta's cold welcome. He knew Arleta had reason to feel the way she did so he couldn't bring himself to blame her. But that didn't keep him from feeling helpless and frustrated.

Big Red snorted and shook his head. His long auburn mane rippled and the harness jangled. "*Ya*, I know, big guy. Time to get back to some oats, ain't so?" Vernon began to imagine a big platter of roast beef, mashed potatoes and roasted carrots. "Wouldn't mind a *gut* meal myself." Vernon patted Big Red on his muscled neck as he daydreamed about the food Sadie might be preparing. He sure did appreciate a home-cooked meal after so many months of living off canned foods and sandwiches.

Vernon was so busy daydreaming he didn't pay attention to his surroundings, working his way through the familiar fields and pasturelands on autopilot. Then, when he reached the farmyard, his attention snapped into place and he stopped short. Big Red tried to keep walking and yanked hard on the harness, but Vernon didn't budge. He couldn't believe what he saw.

The yard was immaculate. The dead grass had been mowed. The rubbish and weeds had disappeared. The hedges lining the farmhouse had been neatly trimmed and he could see the chipped windowsills for the first time in months. The window panes, now fully visible, had been scrubbed clean. The entire property had been reborn, as if the past had been swept away.

It was unacceptable.

"Daed!" Ned and Newt raced to him in a whirlwind of grins and shouts. "Look what we did!" Lydia trotted after them. "I helped too, *Daed*!" Vernon tried to force a smile, but his heart had dropped into his gut at the sight of the yard. He managed a slow nod. *"Ya.* I see that."

"But *Daed*," Lydia tugged on the sleeve of his blue work shirt. "Aren't you happy?"

The confused, crestfallen look on her face made his heart drop even farther. "Of course I am," he said.

"Then why do you look so upset?"

Vernon realized he was scowling and tried to soften his expression. "I'm not upset. You did a *gut* job." An image of Lorna kneeling in front of her kitchen garden overwhelmed him. It was all he could see. "I have to go," he said as he stumbled past his children. He caught a glimpse of Sadie's face as he rushed past. Her mouth was open in surprise, her forehead crinkled in concern. Or perhaps in judgment. Her expression cut deeply and he found himself lashing back. "I didn't hire you to do yard work," he said as he stalked past. "You should be getting dinner on. That's what I hired you to do."

He felt a stab of guilt even as he said the words and wished he could take them back. But now it was too late and he was afraid that if he opened his mouth again, he would only make it worse. Vernon knew he ought to stop, apologize to Sadie, then hug his children and thank them for what they did today. But he was afraid the tears would come if he did. He had to be strong. He had to keep pushing the grief and guilt down or it might overtake them all. So he kept his head down and walked away.

Vernon avoided his family until he had to join them at the kitchen table. The meal was strained and silent. There was so much Vernon wanted to say—knew he needed to say— but couldn't. And the longer he waited, the more impossible it seemed to broach the subject. Only Arleta seemed un- affected; she rarely spoke at meals anyway, unless it was to criticize. Her eyes cut to the generous scoops of ice cream— and sprinkles and chocolate sauce—on the children's plates and she shook her head. "What is this? Ice cream for sup- per?"

Sadie nodded but didn't look up.

"Vernon, this isn't acceptable." Arleta pointed a finger at Sadie. "Don't you know *kinner* have to eat their vege- tables before they can have dessert? What kind of *kinns- maad* are you?"

Sadie swallowed hard, then raised her chin. Vernon could see she was mustering the courage to defend herself. "The kind of *kinnsmaad* that gets these *buwe* to behave," Vernon said before Sadie could get a word in. "Let her be, Arleta," he added in a soft, gentle voice.

"Humph." Arleta narrowed her eyes at Vernon before shoving a big bite of roasted chicken in her mouth and chewing angrily. The children continued to devour their ice cream in silence. The only sound was the swinging of the twins' legs beneath the table and the ticking of the clock on the wall. Arleta swallowed and said, "It's not the way things should be done."

Vernon sighed. "Just because it's different from how we've always done things doesn't mean it's bad. I'm sure Sadie has a reason for it." He cleared his throat and hesitated. "I trust her."

Sadie's eyes shot to Vernon's as a look of surprise overtook her face. Vernon's cheeks burned at her eye contact, but he managed a kind nod before averting his gaze. He could feel Sadie's eyes on him, studying him for a long time afterward.

When dinner was over, Vernon hurried from the table. There were always chores to do in the barn; they would keep him hidden and occupied until bedtime. That way he could put off having to face his guilt until tomorrow. But when Vernon finally left the quiet sanctuary of the barn and headed back to the house, he heard the slow creak of a rocker moving back and forth on the porch. He raised the kerosene lantern, throwing light and shadows up the steps and across the weathered porch. He could make out a woman's silhouette in the shadows. "*Kumme* sit, Vernon," Sadie's voice said from the darkness. "I've got a glass of lemonade for you."

Vernon tried to think of an excuse. The last thing he wanted was to face Sadie after his remarks in the yard earlier that day. "I've got to, uh—"

"You've got to sit and talk about this." There was an awkward pause. "Please," she added softly. He could sense her nervousness and felt admiration for her courage. It wasn't easy to face someone for a difficult conversation—he knew that better than anyone. And he could only imagine how intimidating he must seem, all gruff and raw after so many lonely, harrowing months of suppressed grief and guilt.

He sighed. "Sure, Sadie," he said after a moment, in what he hoped was a gentle tone. "I'll sit with you."

"Danki." He heard the rattle of ice followed by a soft thud of glass hitting wood. As he drew near, her form became clear by the flickering orange glow of his kerosene lantern. Two glasses of lemonade sat on the little table between her and an empty rocking chair. He set the lantern on the table beside the glasses and settled into the empty chair. The wood squeaked beneath his weight.

"I wanted to talk to you…" Sadie's voice faded away and Vernon could see she was struggling to find the right words.

"It's *oll recht*," Vernon said gently. "Go ahead and say what you need to say."

She nodded but didn't speak right away. June bugs buzzed nearby and a lightning bug flashed in the distance. "It's about today," Sadie said finally. She shifted in her chair. "I know I probably shouldn't tell you this, but I feel I can't keep silent. I hope… I hope you understand."

"Go on."

"Your *kinner*. They were so excited to surprise you today. Even the *buwe*." She paused and a faint smile appeared on her lips. "Especially the *buwe*. They wanted to make you happy." She picked up the glass beside her but didn't take a sip. Instead, she turned it in her hands. "I promised them it would make you happy if they did a *gut* job clearing the yard. I let them down. I got their hopes up and…" She didn't finish the sentence. She didn't have to.

"You didn't let them down," Vernon said in a firm voice. "I did."

Sadie's eyes shot to his face. "You see that?"

"Ye." He sighed. "I do. And I'm not proud of it."

"They just want to get your attention," Sadie said. "They just want to know that you love them and want to be a part of their lives." Her eyes dropped and Vernon could tell that she was worried she had said too much. "That's all they want."

The truth cut more deeply than Vernon could handle. "They know that," he retorted gruffly.

Sadie's gaze moved back to his, her blue eyes piercing in their boldness. "Do they?"

Vernon looked down at his hands. "I like to think they do."

"They're *kinner*. They need to be told. They need to see it. They can't infer things the way we can."

Vernon's hand moved to his forehead. He rubbed his temples. "I don't..."

"It's *oll recht*," Sadie said quietly.

"I don't know how to do that anymore." There, he had said it. The admission flooded him with emotion. Vernon squeezed his eyes shut. "I can't do it anymore." Vernon shook his head, his eyes still closed. "The truth is, Lorna used to keep the yard. She loved weeding and planting. She said it calmed her. That's why the yard got so bad after we lost her—I haven't been able to face it because it carries too much of her. It brought it all back today, seeing the yard the way she liked to keep it. I couldn't handle it, I guess. But I sure couldn't say anything about that to the *kinner*."

"You think you can't. But you can talk to them about how you feel. I know you can." Her hand moved to his arm and she touched him through the sleeve of his shirt for the briefest moment to emphasize her words. He felt the warm comfort of her message conveyed through her fingers before she pulled them away. There was something so reassuring and loving in that soft, brief touch. It had made him feel like he wasn't alone, after all. It had made him feel like he could find his way back to himself again.

Vernon cleared his throat as he set aside his pride. "How do you think I could go about doing that?"

Sadie smiled into the darkness. More lightning bugs flashed in the farmyard beyond the porch railing. "You just say what you feel. It isn't as hard as you think it will be."

Vernon nodded. "Well," he said and rapped the arm of his chair. "I guess I best start with you."

Sadie's face changed to surprise, but she didn't speak.

"I owe you an apology." Vernon cleared his throat again and shifted in his chair. "I, uh, shouldn't have criticized you when I came in from the fields. You did a *gut* job on that yard with the *kinner*. I should have thanked you."

"You were right. You didn't hire me to do yard work."

"You did more than you were hired to do. You went above and beyond. That deserves praise, not contempt. I was rude and there's no excuse."

A slight smile flickered at the edge of Sadie's lips. "*Ya.* That's true."

Vernon managed to give her a playful grin. "I'm glad we agree."

Sadie's smile widened. "Me too."

The atmosphere shifted between them and Vernon felt his throat tighten. He sensed something growing between them, something more than a surface friendship between an employer and his children's nanny.

"Vernon?"

The sound of his voice on her lips sent a strange feeling through him. *"Ya?"*

"Did you mean what you said at supper tonight? That just because something is different from how it's always been done doesn't mean it's bad?"

"*Ya.* I meant it."

"Not many other Amish folks around here think that way."

"Maybe not. But there's plenty of things that make me different from most of the others."

Sadie's brow crinkled. "Like what?"

Reality flooded Vernon's chest in a heavy wave. He shook his head. "Nothing. It's not important." He stood up suddenly, making the empty chair rock back and forth. "I should go." No one else in Bluebird Hills was responsible for his wife's death or his sister's disability. Vernon was different in a way that set him apart forever. Different in a way that could never be forgiven.

Whatever bond had begun to form between them, Vernon had to sever it. He owed that much to Sadie. She deserved far better than he could ever give.

Chapter Six

Sadie walked into an empty kitchen the next morning. The soft murmur of voices filtered through the floor above her. She needed to get the twins up and out the door to help Vernon with the morning chores. The livestock had to be cared for, even though it was the Sabbath. But, after trotting up the stairs, she heard Vernon's deep voice coming from their room. "You did a *gut* job yesterday and you made me happy. I should have told you that yesterday."

"Did I make you happy too?" Lydia's voice piped up. "I raked leaves all by myself with my little rake. The one you got me at the hardware store that's made just for *kinner*."

"You made me very happy, Lydia. You all did."

Sadie cleared her throat to announce her presence as she neared the doorway. *"Gude Mariye."*

"Ah. You're up." Vernon smiled and Lydia bounced in his lap. *"Gude Mariye."*

"Gude Mariye, Sadie," the twins said. For the first time, it seemed like they meant what they said to her, without any secret motives or mischief. Their faces seemed a little brighter and their shoulders a little straighter this morning. Sadie smiled. Their father's words had had a strong effect on them. "I didn't realize I overslept. I'm sorry."

"Ne, you didn't oversleep. I was eager to talk to the *kinner* this morning." Vernon's eyes communicated an unspo-

ken understanding between them. "I had some important things to tell them."

Sadie blushed and looked away. She had never felt this confused about a man before. Last night she had been sure that they had formed some sort of unexpected connection, but then Vernon had abruptly cut it off and walked away so fast she was afraid she had offended him. Sadie had tossed and turned all night, worried that she had said too much—or too little. But then, this morning, he had taken her advice.

It was all so bewildering.

Vernon kissed the top of Lydia's head, slid her off his lap and stood up. "Time to get going, *ya*?"

Lydia bounced up from the bed. "Where are we going?"

Vernon shrugged, but his eyes twinkled, showing he knew this was out of the ordinary. "It's a visiting Sunday, ain't so?"

"But we never go visiting!" Lydia said. The twins looked at one another then leaped up. "Let's go!" they shouted.

"What a *gut* idea, Vernon," Sadie said.

Vernon looked down and studied a crack in the hardwood floor. "*Ach*, as you well know, it wasn't my idea. Just taking everyone's advice and trying to do what's right."

Sadie smiled. "This is going to be a wonderful day."

The children had never dressed and eaten breakfast as quickly as they did that morning. The only complication was cajoling Arleta into coming along. She insisted on staying behind to spend the day alone in the shadowy interior of the *dawdi haus*. But Lydia begged her to come with such sweet sincerity that Arleta finally threw up her hands and climbed into the back of the buggy alongside her niece and nephews.

The buggy horse, Old Max, pulled them swiftly along the narrow lanes of Bluebird Hills. After the morning's conversation between Vernon and his children, the world felt ripe with possibilities and Sadie couldn't help but notice how close his elbow was to hers as he held the reins. She felt a little zap of excitement to be in the front seat beside him, the wind whipping the fabric of her dress and the sun warming her face. The golden rays brightened the fields of alfalfa hay and barley, nearly ripe for the harvest. Holstein cows dotted green pastures against a backdrop of red barns, weathered white silos and gently rolling hills. Children dressed in their freshly ironed Sunday best walked hand in hand along the back roads. Other people passed by in buggies, waving as they rumbled along toward their own friends and families.

Sadie took a deep breath of the warm summer air and exhaled. For the first time since she had taken the job as the Kauffman's nanny, she felt a sense of peace and rightness. Maybe everything would be okay after all.

"We'll go to your house, *ya*?" Vernon asked Sadie as he held the reins, his eyes on the road ahead.

"Ya!" a chorus of cheers rose from the back seat.

"We want to see Sadie's family," Lydia said.

Vernon nodded. "It's decided then."

"Danki, Vernon. That sounds *wunderbar*. I can't wait to see them again. I've only been gone a few days, but it's the longest we've ever been apart. It's funny because I used to daydream about getting away all the time—my younger *brudres* and *schwester* used to drive me crazy, you know." Sadie smiled and shook her head. "You don't appreciate what you have until it's gone."

Vernon didn't respond. Instead, his expression tightened.

Sadie felt a pang of discomfort. She had said the wrong thing. Vernon's wounds were still so fresh and raw that just about anything could rub them open again. She turned away and looked out over the green and yellow fields, laid out beyond the road in a checkerboard of waving grain. Vernon couldn't keep holding on to all that loss. He had to find a way to heal. But what could she do about it?

When they arrived at Sadie's yellow farmhouse, the property was quiet, the yard empty. The silence was uncharacteristic of her boisterous family. "They've gone visiting," Sadie said to Vernon. "But the buggy's still here. They must be at the Millers' next door. They would have cut across the middle pasture by foot."

Vernon nodded and clicked his tongue at Old Max. "Walk on."

In addition to a large farm, Levi and Katie Miller owned a souvenir shop and farm stand that tourists adored. As they neared, a big sign came into view alongside the highway with the words Aunt Fannie's Amish Gifts in giant red letters. Beneath the words were colorful images of assorted wares, from quilts and cookies to fresh vegetables and faceless Amish dolls. Sadie smiled. She had painted the sign to help the Millers drum up business and save the shop, back when sales had been down and they almost had to close. It was one of the first times that she had felt that *Gott* could use her skills as an artist. In fact, the day she painted that sign was when she began to believe that her art wasn't a temptation, but a gift. Conformity was valued among the Amish, and being born with a creative spirit had not been easy for Sadie.

Beyond the big wooden sign sat a quaint little building with a tin roof and gingerbread trim painted pink, white and blue. Sadie had helped pick the color scheme for the renovation of the building and now it looked like an oversize Victorian dollhouse. She felt a surge of pride at the design and had to resist the sin of *hoochmut,* which, as Plain people, the Amish avoided above all else. That was the problem with being an artist, her community insisted. Creating art tempted one to pride because it put attention on the artist instead of on God.

But what if Sadie could use her art for good, like she had done for the Millers, to help save their livelihood? What if she could find a way to help other people using the gift God had given her? She pondered this as Vernon pulled the reins and Old Max veered left, into the gravel parking lot beside the shop, the wheels crunching over the uneven ground.

The bishop's buggy was already parked in the lot and Vernon pulled alongside it, near a hitching post for Amish visitors. Vernon hopped down and hurried to tie Old Max's lead so he could graze alongside the bishop's horse on a strip of grass beyond the gravel parking lot. Then Vernon helped Sadie down from her seat. Their eyes met briefly and Sadie had to look away because the touch of his hand felt too comfortable, too safe. Vernon Kauffman was not supposed to make her feel that way.

"Look!" Sadie said as her feet hit the ground. She squinted into the sun. "It's my younger *brudres*." Three boys sat on a bale of hay in the farmyard, in front of a big red barn. A tall silo and squat grain bin stood in the distance, surrounded by rolling hills of fields and pastureland. Overlooking a pond beyond the barn, the blades of a red windmill turned in the lazy, humid breeze.

The boys jumped up when they saw the buggy and trotted toward Sadie. Levi's son, Simon, appeared from behind the barn and ran to catch up. He clutched a ball in one hand and adjusted his thick glasses with the other.

Ned and Newt scrambled over Lydia and were out of the buggy before Sadie could even get out a hello. She managed to steal a hug from one of her brothers before they dashed away with Vernon's sons and Simon, disappearing beyond the big red barn. Vernon chuckled. "Looks like the day is off to a *gut* start."

"For certain sure," Sadie answered with a smile.

Lydia climbed down from her seat and hurried after her brothers. "Don't worry." Anna, the second eldest Lapp sister, jogged toward the buggy. "I'll keep an eye on her while I'm out here watching our younger *brudres* and *schwester*. Go inside and visit with *Mamm* and *Daed*. They'll be so happy to see you." Sadie gave Anna a quick, happy hug before Anna trotted after Lydia and the rest of the younger children.

Arleta had not spoken a word during the entire ride, and her lips stayed tightly pursed as she lowered herself from the back seat of the buggy and brushed off the skirt of her purple Sunday dress. Sadie thought she caught a glimmer of vulnerability in the woman's eyes as she gazed at the sprawling, white farmhouse in front of them, but the expression was quickly replaced by a frown. "Let's not stay long," Arleta said. "Those *kinner* are sure to get up to foolishness."

"I'm sure it'll be fine, Arleta," Vernon murmured.

Arleta let out a little humph, straightened her *kapp* and headed toward the wraparound porch, her chin raised like a soldier readying for battle.

Vernon's palms felt sweaty and his heart beat too hard in his chest. It had been so long since he had been sociable that he no longer felt comfortable around his own people anymore. He lifted his black Sunday hat, smoothed down his dark brown hair and replaced the hat. He cut his eyes toward Arleta, careful not to move his head so she wouldn't suspect that he was worriedly watching her. Her lips were tight, her face a blank mask. He knew she was anxious about going inside a crowded room. They both were. Vernon because he couldn't live down the shame, and

Arleta because she didn't want anyone to know how hard she struggled after her head injury.

Sadie's grin was the only thing that kept him going. If she hadn't been strolling beside him with those shining eyes, he would have turned, slunk back to the buggy and raced home to hide.

As they walked into the Millers' living room, Vernon felt an almost imperceptible touch on his arm. Had Sadie just given him a gesture of reassurance? Or had she accidently brushed him as they passed through the doorway? He suspected that the touch had been intentional. He could tell that Sadie was the kind of person who could sense another's need and offer comfort. But to offer *him* comfort, after the walls he had tried to put between them? He didn't know what to make of that. He only knew that it made him feel warm and safe, deep inside.

Vernon frowned as he fought to regain control of his thoughts. He couldn't feel that way about Sadie. She was too bright and lovely for him to even dream of courting. He would taint her with the shame of what he had done on that terrible night of the buggy accident. Even now, he could barely face walking into a room of Amish brothers and sisters. How could he dare to imagine a connection with such a good woman?

The room erupted with noise as everyone rose to greet them. Arleta visibly flinched. Amos was the first to reach Vernon. The bishop gave him a hearty slap on the back. "*Gut* to see you take an old man's advice," he said with a wink.

"*Ach*, you were right," Vernon said. "The *kinner* need to get out more."

Amos raised an eyebrow. "Only the *kinner*?"

Vernon was glad he didn't have to answer. Instead, he was swept into the happy chaos of Sadie's big family as they swarmed her for hugs and news of her life on the Kauffman farm. Arleta withdrew from the fray and inched backward, toward the far wall. Vernon managed to slip over to her and put a hand on her elbow. "It's *oll recht*."

"I know it's *oll recht*," Arleta snapped. "I'm perfectly fine."

Vernon nodded but kept his hand on her elbow. She didn't try to shake it off and Vernon knew that, despite her protests, she needed him there.

After a few minutes the noise level settled down to a low hum and everyone found a seat. Levi Miller plopped down on a wooden crate that had copies of the *Budget* newspaper stacked inside. Vernon led Arleta to a row of folding chairs that had been set out for visitors, then sat down beside Katie Miller and Sadie's father, Abram. Bishop Amos, Edna and Sadie took a seat on the battered blue couch, while Sadie's mother, Ada, settled into the rocking chair with a gurgling baby in her lap. Ada was plump, had salt-and-pepper hair tucked beneath her *kapp*, and her eyes shone as she gazed across the room at her daughter.

"So, tell us everything, Sadie," Ada said. "I'm sure the *kinner* are very happy to have you there. And Vernon and Arleta too." She glanced at Vernon, then to Arleta as she said their names.

Vernon nodded, but Arleta frowned. Vernon nudged her in the ribs. But she just sat there and stared. Ada's face fell and she looked away quickly.

"Uh, *ya*, Sadie has been a very *gut* worker," Vernon said. Then he leaned in close to Arleta's ear and whispered, "Tell them you're glad to have Sadie."

"Nee," she said, her voice audible for the rest of the room to hear.

Vernon inched closer to his sister's ear. "Shhhh. You'll give them the wrong idea."

"I won't lie, Vernon. You know that's a sin."

Vernon groaned inside. "Arleta, please. Just be nice."

"Then I won't say anything. Because you know, if you haven't got anything nice to say, then you shouldn't say anything at all."

"Shhhh, Arleta. Please take some care! They'll hear you."

Vernon pulled away from his sister to see every face in the room staring at them. He swallowed hard. Arleta might not have said everything she was thinking, but she had said enough—and it was clear the entire room had heard. Vernon wanted to sink into the floor and disappear. Abram glared at him and Bishop Amos had an expression of disappointment. Worst of all was seeing Sadie's face. She looked like she might cry. But she pushed the emotion down and announced in her most cheerful voice, "Ned and Newt have been a handful, but they are sweet, *gut buwe*."

Vernon recognized that Sadie was changing the subject to take the attention off him and Arleta. He felt a wave of gratitude. Even when stung from rejection, she continued to think of others. Could anyone truly have such a kind heart?

Abram leaned forward slightly and narrowed his eyes. "Newt? Who is this Newt?"

Sadie chuckled. "*Ach*, that's Jonathon Kauffman, *Daed*. He goes by Newt."

"Why?" Abram gave Vernon a look of firm disapproval. "Why would a *bu* go by such a name?"

"Because he won't go by anything else," Sadie explained.

Vernon could see the direction this was headed and knew that Sadie's attempt to help was actually going to make the situation worse. Abram was not a man who approved of imaginative or strong-willed children.

"Why don't you make him go by his real name?" Abram asked as he stared at Vernon.

Vernon shifted in his seat. There was so much to explain that he couldn't possibly say to a crowd of people. After Newt lost his mother, Vernon wanted to do everything he could to comfort his son. If that meant calling him by a silly nickname, so be it. He would go to the moon and back for Newt, if that would help. Letting the boy take back a little control over his life by renaming himself was the least Vernon could do to support the grieving child. Maybe he was wrong to be so lenient, but he didn't know. He had never had to comfort a motherless child before. Most men never did. There was no road map.

"Why not?" Vernon said at last. It was the best explanation he could think of without giving away how he really felt. "It's not hurting anyone."

Abram snorted. "It's hurting the boy to allow him to be headstrong and to bring attention on himself. *Kinner* need a firm hand."

Abram and Vernon both turned to Amos for support. "What do you think, Bishop?" Abram asked.

"I think we should let Sadie finish her story. This is a conversation for another time. Not a visiting Sunday."

Vernon gave a grateful nod. Abram did not look pleased, but he did not contradict his Bishop.

"Well, as I was saying," Sadie continued, flashing the room with her bright smile. Vernon nearly forgot the awkward moment when he saw Sadie's expression light up the room. "Ned and Newt have been up to some *lecherich* antics since I arrived.*"

"Lecherich?" Abram asked. "How ridiculous?"

Sadie's face froze for an instant and Vernon could tell that she had recognized her mistake. Her no-nonsense father would not be amused by her story, no matter how sweet and endearing she made it. Vernon had a sinking feeling that this visiting Sunday had been a bad idea.

"*Ach*, not too *lecherich*," Sadie said quickly. "Just ridiculous enough to be cute."

Abram did not look like he agreed.

Ada shifted the baby in her arms and said, "Go on, Sadie. I'd like to hear your story. You always tell *gut* stories."

Sadie grinned. "Well, the most ridiculous thing they did was hide a snake in my bed."

Ada gasped. "A snake!" The baby began to cry at his mother's outburst and she jostled him in her arms. "Shhhh. It's *oll recht*," she whispered to the baby. "I just got surprised, is all."

"Not a real one, *Mamm*!"

Ada chuckled. "*Gut* to know."

"Sorry, I should have made that clear. But, as I was saying, I found a snake—a toy snake—but I thought it was real. I screamed so loudly that Vernon came running all the way from the farmhouse. Then he thought it was a real snake too and—"

"Vernon's *buwe* put a toy snake in your bed?" Abram interrupted.

"*Ya*. I was getting to that, but the funny part is—"

"There is nothing funny about misbehaving *buwe*," Abram said.

"*Ya*, but in this case—"

"*Ne*." Abram shook his head. "There are no exceptions to that rule."

As if on cue, Vernon heard the back door fling open and footsteps pound through the kitchen. He cringed as he imagined what might happen next. Ned and Newt burst into the living room, dripping wet and brimming with agitated energy. "Ned pushed me into the pond!" Newt shouted.

"*Ne!* Newt pushed *me* into the pond," Ned retorted.

"Did not!"

"Did too!"

Arleta clapped her hands over her ears at the sudden noise.

Vernon leaped up. "*Buwe!* Quiet down. And go back outside. You're dripping all over Katie's rug."

Every eye in the room moved to the floor where Katie's braided rag rug lay. Water streamed from the twins' black trousers and tousled hair onto the light blue fabric.

"I'm sorry, Katie," Vernon said. "I'll wash it for you…" He felt so flustered he didn't know what to say.

"*Nee*, it's only water, Vernon," Katie said. "As long as the *buwe* aren't hurt."

Vernon felt a tug on his arm.

"I have to go, Vernon," Arleta whispered. Her voice sounded hoarse and alarmed.

Vernon spun around. He didn't know where to put his attention. Everyone needed him in this moment, it seemed. "What's wrong?" he asked in a low voice. But he already knew. Arleta's head injury made her sensitive to noise, light, crowds—any kind of stimulation. All the commotion had set her over the edge.

And it was his fault. She would never have been injured if it weren't for him.

Vernon had to take care of Arleta and deal with his *buwe* and get Katie's floors cleaned up. *"Oll recht,"* Vernon said in his most soothing tone of voice. "Let's get you home." Then he turned to the *buwe*. "You're ruining Katie's house with all that pond water. Get it cleaned up."

"But he pushed me!" Newt shouted. "What about that?"

Arleta's hand tightened on his arm. "Get me out of here," she hissed.

Vernon felt everyone in the room staring at him. He

needed to deal with his sons—and Katie's floors—but the most important thing was to take care of his sister. He knew she was at her breaking point and he had to protect her. She wouldn't be able to bear it if anyone knew the extent of her injuries. She hated to seem weak or incapable.

"We're leaving!" Vernon said, a little too loudly. He was so flustered he didn't know how to explain himself, or the situation, so he just put a firm arm around Arleta to shield her from the stares and barreled out of the room.

Sadie leaped up. She could see that Arleta needed help. And those twins needed to get cleaned up along with Katie's floors. "I'm coming," she shouted after Vernon. "I'll get the *buwe*!" Sadie turned to Katie. "Do you have an old towel or two?"

"Of course. Simon gets in plenty of messes around here." Her stepson was known for his love of animals—especially the kinds that lived in mud and pond scum. Sadie smiled, despite the stress she felt. "I bet he does." Then she peered around the doorway to see Vernon and Arleta disappearing into the kitchen. A moment later, the back door opened and slammed shut. Sadie flinched at the sound. What had gotten into Vernon? She knew that Arleta could get overwhelmed, and the twins were a handful, but he had run out of there as if a pack of wolves were chasing him.

"I'll be back in a minute," Katie said and headed toward the laundry room.

Sadie snapped back to the present. *"Danki."*

Abram stood up and marched toward Sadie. She could feel the disapproval coming off him in waves. "I don't like this, Sadie," he said when he reached her, in a voice too low for the others to hear.

"It's *oll recht, Daed.*"

"Is it?" Abram asked in a stern voice.

Sadie looked down and picked at a thread on her white apron. "*Ya*. That family, they've been through a lot."

"*Ya*. I know of their troubles. But their troubles aren't *your* troubles." Abram sighed. "I know you think I'm too hard sometimes."

Sadie's eyes shot up to his. She had not expected to hear that.

"But it's because it's my duty to protect you and the rest of my *kinner*. Do you understand?"

Her father didn't usually explain himself, and Sadie felt her heart softening toward him. She thought for a moment. "I do. But what does that have to do with what just happened?"

Abram looked surprised. "Because I have to keep you safe."

It took a moment for her to understand. "From Vernon?"

"I'm afraid he's a bad influence, Sadie. The whole family..." Abram shook his head. His expression was of sadness, rather than condemnation. "I know you want to help, Sadie. But some people can't be helped. It's not your job."

"But it is my job, *Daed*."

"*Nee*. Your job is to be a *kinnsmaad*, not a healer. That's too much to ask."

"But, *Daed*, what if it's what I want to do?"

"*Ach*, Sadie. Your heart aches for everyone around you. But if you give and give to everyone who is hurting, what will be left of you? You have to be harder in order to protect yourself. Not everyone can be saved."

Sadie considered that. She put a hand on her father's arm. "I think they can be, *Daed*."

Abram shook his head. His eyes looked sad. "*Ach*, Sadie. That *gut* heart of yours will be the end of you."

Katie swept into the room with a stack of old towels in

her arms. "Here we go," she said and pushed them into the twins' hands. "Dry yourselves off and then wipe down the floors. They'll be *gut* as new in no time."

"But we don't want to," Ned said.

Sadie shot him a look, then asked, "So you want baked beans for dinner?"

Ned and Newt groaned but got to work on the floor.

Sadie turned back to her *Daed*. "I believe I can do *gut* at the Kauffmans'. Even if I can't, I have to try."

"I don't want you to go back. *Kumme* home with us. If you're so set on working, we'll find another job for you. Maybe at the Beilers' quilt shop. The Beilers are *gut* people."

"The Beilers don't need me, *Daed*."

Abram sighed. "I can see you're set on this."

"I am."

Abram studied Sadie as he ran his fingers through his beard. "I could make you come home with us, but I'm not going to. I can see your heart is in the right place. But I don't like it." Abram shook his head. "I think you're going to learn a lesson from this, and it's going to be a difficult one. This won't turn out the way you think, Sadie. I hope you're prepared for that."

"I'm going to trust *Gott* to guide me."

Abram's fingers worked slowly through his beard as the twins shouted and jostled in the background. The adults in the room chatted quietly among themselves. Probably about Vernon's speedy exit, Sadie thought.

Abram stared at his daughter, as if trying to read her mind. "Then you'll realize you don't have the power to fix the Kauffmans."

"But *Gott* does," Sadie finished for him.

Abram lifted his hands, palms up. "Only if Vernon allows it. You can lead a horse to water, but you can't make it drink."

Sadie nodded. "Thank you for letting me stay."

"I'm only allowing it for one month."

"One month! But that's not enough time."

"It's the time I'm giving you."

"Please, *Daed*. What if I'm able to make a difference? Would you let me stay longer then?"

Abram stared down at his daughter, considering. Finally, he nodded, and Sadie exhaled. She had not realized she had been holding her breath. "You may stay longer if I see changes in Vernon," Abram said. "If not, I'm bringing you home for your own *gut*. It won't do for you to be under his influence if his heart is bad."

"His heart isn't bad, *Daed*. It's just…hurting." Sadie felt her own heart ache at the words. She wanted so badly to draw out Vernon's pain and smooth away his past.

Abram's expression hardened. "We all saw his behavior today, Sadie. First he and Arleta whisper rudely, as if we weren't in the room. And then she said things loud enough for us to hear that made it clear she doesn't want you there. His *buwe* run wild, and then he runs out of here without a word." Abram shook his head. "Forget about the state of his heart. It's his actions that matter and I don't like what I see."

Sadie knew there was nothing she could say to convince her father. She was just thankful he was giving her another month with Vernon.

But how could she make a difference in such a short amount of time?

Chapter Seven

Vernon disappeared as soon as they arrived back at his farm. He didn't know what to say to Sadie. It had surprised him that, after he had fled the Millers' living room, she had appeared at the buggy alongside Ned and Newt and climbed inside as though nothing had happened. He had not spoken the entire ride home and he did not intend to start now. All he wanted was to hide and nurse his wounds.

With Arleta safely tucked into the calm and quiet *dawdi haus* to recover from the overstimulation, Vernon was free to head to his own safe place. He slipped into the barn and breathed in deeply, inhaling the familiar, earthy scent of mud, animals and hay. Big Red whinnied and shook his head, sending his mane rippling. An oversized hoof stomped on the floor of his stall.

Vernon smiled. "*Oll recht, oll recht*. I hear you, *bu*." He pulled a few sugar cubes from a tin bucket on the floor and headed over to the draft horse. "How was your day off? Did you enjoy your rest, or has it made you restless?" Big Red snorted and stomped his hoof again. "*Ach*, you just want your sugar cube, *ya*?" Vernon flattened his hand and held it out, palm up. "Quit yapping and give me my food. That's what you're thinking, ain't so?"

Big Red swung his head over the stall door and lowered

his mouth to Vernon's hand. His lips tickled Vernon's skin and made him chuckle. The horse gobbled the sugar cube, then ran his velvety soft lips over Vernon's palm again. He snorted, raised his head and shoved his muzzle into Vernon's chest. The big horse was powerful enough to push Vernon back a step, despite Vernon's height and strength.

"Hey, now. That's all I got, *bu*." Vernon gave the horse a strong pat on the neck. "Settle down, *ya*?"

Big Red whinnied in response. Vernon answered him with another good pat. "You're a *gut* horse, you know that?"

"I didn't know you were so *gut* with animals." It was Sadie's voice.

Vernon swung around to see her standing behind him.

"I'm sorry, I didn't mean to sneak up on you. You must not have heard me *kumme* in."

"Nee." Vernon shuffled from one foot to the other. He didn't like that Sadie had seen him being himself. It felt too vulnerable. Not to mention how embarrassed he felt after his hasty exit from the Millers'. "I didn't."

"Can I pet him?" Sadie looked up at Big Red. He stared down at her with his large black eyes framed with thick eyelashes.

"Ye. But if you really want to win him over, give him a sugar cube. I'll grab you one." Vernon walked to the metal bucket that he kept just out of eyeshot of Big Red's stall. "Big Red loves them so much that I keep them around— but not too close to him."

"You're a softie," Sadie said. "Even though you pretend not to be."

"Ach, Nee. I don't know about that." Vernon frowned and cleared his throat. As soon as he walked back to the stall, Big Red snorted and lunged for the sugar. "Whoa, now, big fella. Sadie's going to give it to you." He pressed the sugar

cube into Sadie's palm. "Here." Her skin was so soft and warm that he felt suddenly befuddled. He cleared his throat again and pulled away from her. "Uh, he's a *gut* horse. Has a mind of his own, but that's not a bad thing."

Sadie grinned and held out her hand, palm up. Big Red grabbed the sugar cube almost instantly. She laughed and wiped her palm on her apron. "Not all Amish would agree with you. Anything with a mind of its own can be threatening, ain't so? To our ways, I mean."

Vernon gave her a sideways glance. "Are you talking about more than horses?"

"Maybe."

Vernon knew that Sadie was an artist. He wondered if she was talking about herself. Or was she talking about him? He wasn't sure what he should say. Vernon let out a deep breath. He had to start somewhere. "Look, about today…"

Sadie nodded encouragingly.

"I, uh…" He picked at a rough patch of wood on the wall of Big Red's stall.

"It's *oll recht*, Vernon. Just say what you need to say."

Sadie's expression was so encouraging, so kind, that it actually made it harder for Vernon to speak. How could such a sweet woman understand what he had done? How could she relate? He took a deep breath and tried to find the words. "I guess it didn't make sense, how Arleta and I ran out of the Millers' today. And before that, we were whispering about you." Vernon shook his head. "None of it went the way I meant for it to."

"What did you mean then?"

"Well, I was encouraging Arleta to be nice when we were whispering. I was telling her to say she likes having you here. But you know Arleta…"

"I'm trying to, Vernon. But she's not easy to understand."

Vernon nodded. "Right. She doesn't mean to come across the way she does. She's just frustrated because she can't do the things she used to do. She longs for her independence. You represent what she lost, because you've taken over the jobs she would be doing if she hadn't been in the accident."

Big Red nudged Vernon's shoulder and he patted the horse absently. "She doesn't always notice what she's doing or how she comes across. She didn't realize how loud she was speaking today. And I know I shouldn't have been whispering in front of other people, but what else could I do? I had to try to help. I didn't want her to hurt you."

Sadie's brow crinkled. "So all that whispering was because you were defending me?"

Vernon's eyes jerked to Sadie. "*Ya.* Of course. What else would I have been doing?"

"*Ach*, I don't know. I wasn't sure…" Sadie looked down and picked at a loose thread on her white apron. "I thought maybe you didn't want me here either." Her voice dropped so that Vernon had to strain to hear her. "Sometimes it seems that way."

Vernon put his hand on her arm and her gaze shot back up to his. He felt desperate to make her understand. "*Nee*, Sadie. I want you here. The problem is me, not you. That's what I'm trying to tell you." Their eyes locked and Vernon could hear the fast, shallow rhythm of her breath. They stared at one another for a tense moment that sent flutters through his belly.

He realized that he shouldn't have touched her arm. She might get the wrong idea. He just wanted to reassure her, to help her see that he meant what he was saying. He dropped his hand and his eyes. "I'm sorry, Sadie. I don't know how to explain."

"Just keep trying."

"You know Arleta struggles because of her traumatic brain injury. But no one sees it. It's an invisible disability that affects her every second of the day. She can never get away from it. But other people don't understand. They think she should just be able to carry on like everyone else. But she can't. That's why I got her out of there fast. She was overwhelmed and needed relief. She gets overstimulated easily. People don't know what that feels like."

Vernon threw up his hands. "I don't even understand, not really, because I've never experienced it. But I can see how hard it makes her life. When we go out, it can seem like she's being unsociable, but really she's just struggling to process the conversation and manage all the sensory input. It got to be too much for her and it's my responsibility to take care of her, so I had to leave without explaining why. I guess everyone thought I was just storming out of there for no *gut* reason."

"I don't know what everyone else thought, and I don't think it matters anyway. But I do know what *I* thought—I trusted that there was more going on than I could see."

Vernon let out a long, slow breath. "I don't know what to say. I didn't expect you to understand."

"You underestimate me."

Vernon flinched. "*Nee*. Never. It just seems…too *gut* to be true."

Sadie laughed and the carefree sound helped ease the tension from Vernon's body. "I've got plenty wrong with me, Vernon. You'll find that out soon enough. I'm definitely not too *gut* to be true."

Vernon raised an eyebrow in disagreement but didn't respond. If he did, it might sound like he was sweet on her.

"What I don't understand, Vernon, is why you feel so responsible for Arleta. I know she's your sister, but the weight you carry for her…" Sadie frowned as she searched for the words. "It just seems like there's more to it, that's all."

The moment that he dreaded had come. There was no hiding from it now. "There is." Vernon leaned his elbows onto the top of the stall door and looked into the distance. He studied the pattern of wood grain on the opposite wall.

"What is it, Vernon?" Sadie prodded gently.

"It's my fault." There. He had said those three terrible words. "It's my fault Arleta was injured." He kept staring at the wall, wishing he could disappear. It took all his strength to say what came next. "And it's my fault that my wife lost her life that night."

Sadie didn't speak for a moment. Vernon knew she would be disturbed by his admission. Now she would leave and never come back. And it would be for the best. He didn't deserve someone so wholesome and good in his life.

"What do you mean, Vernon?" Sadie asked finally. Her voice was even and calm, which he didn't expect.

"It was icy that night. Arleta said we shouldn't go out, but it was the night of the school Christmas pageant and the *kinner* were so disappointed to miss it. The *buwe* had been practicing their lines for weeks and Lydia had been looking forward to it all fall. Lorna had sewn her a new dress and everything. It was the biggest night of the year."

"*Ya*. The Christmas pageant is the most exciting thing that happens in Bluebird Hills. Everyone goes to it."

Vernon nodded. "Arleta and I got into an argument. She said I was being foolish to risk it and I said that I couldn't let down the *kinner* and that she was being overly cautious. And Lorna…" Vernon shook his head. The memory cut so sharply it felt like a physical pain behind his breastbone. "Lorna just looked at me with loving eyes and said, 'Whatever you decide will be the right thing, Vernon. I trust you.'"

"And you made the decision to go."

"Ya." Vernon gave a grim nod. "I did. The *kinner* piled into the back of the buggy—so excited that they were near to bursting. Arleta tried to stop us. She actually shouted at me, then pleaded when I wouldn't budge. I told her she didn't have to come if she was so against it, but she insisted. She said if something bad happened, she wanted to be there for the *kinner* in case they needed her. And Lorna, well, she just climbed right in and smiled up at me as if I couldn't go wrong. She trusted me with her life." He swallowed hard. "And I betrayed her. She would still be here if I hadn't been so prideful as to think that I could drive on icy roads. I figured I knew those roads like the back of my hand and could manage if I was careful. I was wrong."

"What happened?"

"A car slid on the ice and hit us. Thanks be to *Gott* the *kinner* weren't hurt—just a few bruises. But Arleta and Lorna…" He didn't finish the sentence. He didn't need to.

"You couldn't have known, Vernon."

"Of course I could have. Arleta knew. I should have listened to her instead of insisting that I was right." Vernon's hands clenched into fists as they dangled over the stall door. "It was my job to know. It was my job to protect my family."

"You were trying to do the right thing. You just wanted to make the *kinner* happy."

"And instead, I took their *mamm* from them—and their *aenti* too, in a way. She'll never be the same. And it's because she was trying to protect her niece and nephews from my bad decision."

"I think there's still hope for Arleta, Vernon. She's stronger than you realize. Give it more time. She may never be the same again, but *Gott* has a way of making things work for *gut*, despite the worst of circumstances."

"It's hard to see that, Sadie."

"That's why it's called faith and not sight."

Vernon grunted as he let Sadie's words sink in. Then he shook his head and turned to her. "You're being so kind about this. I don't understand. Aren't you ashamed of me now?"

"Ashamed of you? Why?"

"Because…" Vernon waved his hand in an agitated circle. "Because of what I did. I just explained it."

"You just explained that you were a loving *daed* who made the wrong decision with the right intentions."

"I was arrogant, prideful. I should have listened to Arleta."

Sadie took a slow breath in and out. She nodded slowly. "Okay, so you were prideful. But you didn't mean for this to happen. We all make mistakes. This was an accident. It wasn't intentional. You were trying to do the right thing. That matters."

Vernon's jaw flexed. He wanted so badly to believe what Sadie was saying, but he couldn't. Everything in him pushed her message away. He had blamed himself for so long that he couldn't imagine feeling any other way. Besides, didn't he owe it to Lorna and Arleta to feel that crushing load of guilt? How else could he make amends?

"Let it go, Vernon."

"Nee." Vernon felt his resolve strengthen. "I can't. I won't."

Sadie looked as if she didn't understand.

"It's all I have left to give," Vernon whispered.

Sadie's expression changed as the meaning behind his words registered. "Your guilt won't change anything. It won't help anyone."

Vernon felt a hot flush of shame and frustration flare through his body. He pushed away from the stall. He felt too exposed, too raw. It had been a mistake to tell Sadie. He wouldn't be able to hide who he was from her anymore. "I have to go," he said and turned away from her.

"Wait." Sadie's voice faltered. "You don't have to run away."

Vernon didn't respond. He was too busy getting out of there as fast as he could.

Chapter Eight

Sadie expected things to be different between her and Vernon after their conversation in the barn. They weren't. If anything, Vernon was more taciturn and reclusive than ever. He barely looked up during meals and he only murmured a quick *ya* or *nee* when spoken to. Ned, Newt and Lydia chattered enough to fill the silence around the table, but Sadie could still sense the tension.

She managed to catch Vernon coming in from the fields on Wednesday afternoon, after three days of strained silence between them. She was pinning one of Lydia's dresses to the clothesline when she caught sight of him striding in from the north pasture, Big Red's lead in his hand. The enormous draft horse plodded slowly beside him, swishing his tail to keep away the flies. The setting sun hovered behind their silhouettes, painting the sky orange. They both looked tired and Sadie wondered if she should just leave Vernon alone.

No, she had to do something. Especially now that her father had set a deadline on how long she could stay. She hadn't even had a chance to tell Vernon that. "Vernon!" Sadie shouted across the farmyard. She dropped the clothespin in her hand into the clothes basket and made a beeline toward him. Vernon's face tightened as she approached and he gave a curt nod.

"Are you *oll recht*?" Sadie asked.

"*Ya*. Of course. How are you?" He did not slow down or wait for an answer.

Sadie trotted alongside him, trying to keep up. His legs took much longer strides than hers. After a moment of awkward silence, Vernon sighed and stopped. Big Red snorted and stomped a hoof. "What is it, Sadie?" Vernon asked in a tired voice.

"Uh, it's just…" Now that she had Vernon's attention, Sadie had no idea what to say.

"*Ya?* It's just what?"

"I can't work here much longer."

Vernon's jaw clenched and he looked past Sadie, to the fields beyond. *"Oll recht."*

Was that all Vernon was going to say about it? That it was all right? Didn't he want her to stay? Sadie stared at Vernon as she felt her cheeks redden.

"Big Red wants his oats. I best head on to the barn now."

"Wait. Don't you want me to stay?"

Vernon didn't look at her. "It doesn't matter what I want. If you want to go, then you ought to go."

"*Nee*. It's not that. My *daed* wants me home soon. He says I can't stay longer than a month."

Vernon shifted Big Red's lead from one hand to another. "I told you it's *oll recht*. I understand you want to leave."

Frustration flared inside Sadie. "I told you it's not my choice. Don't you believe me?"

Vernon hesitated. He patted Big Red's neck absently, eyes still focused on something far away. "What I believe is that I told you more than I should have Sunday night. I'm sorry. It wasn't right for me to involve you in my life."

"Vernon, what are you so afraid of? What are you running from?"

Vernon's eyebrows slammed down and his eyes cut to Sadie. "I'm not afraid and I'm not running. I'm just doing what's right. You'd do well to go home now instead of waiting until the end of the month."

Sadie's heart pounded in her chest. "Is that what you want?"

Vernon paused. His dark eyes bored into hers until she felt he could see all the way through her. It sent a ripple down her spine. *"Ya,"* he said in a slow, low voice. "It is." And then he tugged Big Red's lead and walked away, the huge horse lumbering behind him.

Sadie did not know what to think or do. Didn't he appreciate what she had done for his family? She had seen such progress since her arrival. Even the twins were better behaved since she had taken the job.

And, perhaps even more remarkably, Sadie had been sure that she and Vernon had had their own breakthrough on Sunday. He had opened up to her and she had felt his pain—before he slammed himself shut, like a book he refused to let her read.

Sadie knew what she needed to do to work through her emotions. After tucking Lydia in and making sure the twins were safe in their beds for the night, Sadie headed to her little room in the *dawdi haus* and pulled a wooden box out from under her bed. She gripped the box tightly and strode into the dimly lit living room, toward the front door. Arleta's glider chair creaked as Sadie walked past, but Arleta didn't say anything. Sadie breathed a sigh of relief as soon as she crossed the room and shut the door firmly behind her. Arleta would never approve of what she was about to do, so Sadie was thankful there hadn't been any questions about where she was going.

Sadie made her way down the rickety steps of the *dawdi*

haus and around the side of the old farmhouse. The giant oak tree stood silhouetted in the moonlight as crickets chirped in the humid darkness. Sadie's bare feet found their way through the yard, to the back door and into the kitchen. She let herself in quietly and felt a weight lift when saw that the house was empty and still. Vernon wouldn't even notice she was there. He had been successfully avoiding her all week and must be asleep by now anyway. She could have an hour to herself, which was exactly what she needed.

Sadie set the wooden box on the kitchen table, flipped the metal latch and opened the lid to reveal tubes of acrylic paint, a handful of paint brushes, a pallet and a small canvas. She ran her fingers over the familiar tubes, feeling as if she had been reunited with old friends. A smile overtook her face as she grabbed an empty Mason jar from a kitchen cabinet, filled it with water and set it down beside the wooden box.

"Now," Sadie said to herself. "Let's get started." She cracked her knuckles, sat down and closed her eyes. She took a moment to feel the emotions that had been boiling inside of her—the frustration and hurt, the confusion and irritation. Vernon had no right to dismiss her the way he had. It was as if he didn't care about her at all. *And why does that bother me so much?* she asked herself. She didn't know. Sadie frowned and opened her eyes. She was ready to paint what she felt. Afterward, it would begin to make sense. It always did.

"Please *Gott*, guide my hand and let this be to Your glory. And help me to feel better afterward. Thank You. Amen." When Sadie began to paint, the strokes were softer and more hesitant than she expected. The colors she instinctively chose were shades of blue and purple—colors of sadness and loss. She had expected more orange and red—

colors of frustration and anger. Her fingers flew without thinking, creating a soft, blurred image of a lone tree. Need and isolation cried out from the canvas.

Sadie lost track of time. She didn't stop until something settled inside of her and she knew that the painting was finished. She set down her paintbrush and studied the canvas. How odd, she thought. She had painted an image that represented Vernon. She had come to get out her own confusion and hurt, but had channeled his instead. She stared at the lone blue tree, surrounded by an empty blue field and a vast purple sky, and felt consumed by the emptiness of the scene.

"What do you think you're doing?" Vernon's voice boomed across the kitchen.

Sadie jumped in her chair. "I, um…" Sadie swallowed hard. "Painting."

Vernon just stared at her.

"Sorry, you startled me." She stood up quickly. "Anyway, I'm finished now. I'll get back to the *dawdi haus*." She began to toss the tubes of paint back into the box. Her fingers fumbled nervously and she dropped a tube onto the floor. "I didn't think Arleta would like me to paint there. I thought this would be better." The silence made her feel like she had to explain herself. Sadie crouched down to pick up the tube she dropped, stood back up and shoved it into the wooden box.

"You shouldn't have painted here either," Vernon said.

Sadie flinched.

"Don't paint in my house again."

Sadie wanted to sink into the floor. She had faced disapproval over her artwork before but, after getting to know Vernon, she thought that he shared her need to push the boundaries, to find her way to God even when it made the rest of the church district uncomfortable. They couldn't understand that God had given her the talent to paint and that she did it to feel close to Him and make sense of things that she couldn't decipher in words.

But now, Sadie realized that Vernon was the same as the rest of them.

Vernon couldn't believe he had ordered Sadie not to paint in his house. He felt like an ogre even as he said the words. But it had come pouring out of him instinctively, before he could stop himself. He had seen her painting and felt so moved by it that he had to shut down inside—and shut down what had made him feel such strong emotion.

Sadie and her painting had to go.

"What is that? What have you painted?" Vernon asked as he stared at the isolated tree beneath a vast, lonely sky, all of it depicted in riveting shades of blue and purple. He wanted to look away, but couldn't. Something inside of him felt connected to that painting. He understood the isolation it conveyed, the desolation, the utter feeling of loss, as if no one else in the entire world existed anymore.

"It's nothing," Sadie stammered. She knocked over the Mason jar of water as she hurried to collect her supplies. "I'm sorry!" She darted to the counter, grabbed an old dishrag and ran back to the table.

Vernon realized how disapproving he must seem, looming over her with his usual frown on his face. He sighed. Would he ever figure out how to do better? "It's *oll recht*," Vernon said in a voice that he hoped sounded gentle enough. "Just an accident."

Sadie nodded but didn't look up. She attacked the puddle of water with all her attention. "Here," Vernon said. "Let me." He reached for the cloth but caught her hand instead as she slid it against the table.

She glanced up, her cheeks blooming red.

"Sorry. I just…" Vernon cleared his throat and gently moved his hand to take the dishrag from her. "I'll take care of this." He hoped she understood that this was his way of apologizing. He hadn't meant to be a brute. But that painting brought up too many emotions. Especially after their conversation on Sunday. He had been avoiding her ever since. He wasn't proud of that fact, but what else could he do? He felt too exposed to do anything different. She knew the worst of him now, and all he could think when he looked into her sweet, innocent eyes was that he was a villain who shouldn't burden her with the mistake that had destroyed his family.

So he refused to look into those eyes.

All week, he had kept his head down and his mouth shut, stewing in his shame.

Sadie banged the lid of the box shut and snapped the latch. She opened her mouth to speak, then shut it again. A trace of confusion and disappointment crossed her face and Vernon had to look away. He couldn't believe he had made her feel that way. "What is it?" he asked. "What did you want to say?" The least he could do was give her a chance to tell him how she felt. He deserved to be criticized.

Sadie looked down at the box in her hand. Her knuckles tightened around the handle. "I…"

"Go on," Vernon encouraged, expecting her to tell him that she would leave tomorrow. He wouldn't argue with her. No, he had to face the fact that she was right. He had pushed everyone away since the accident and now it was too late to stop. He didn't know how to connect with anyone anymore after so much brokenness.

"I thought you saw the world like I do," Sadie said softly, eyes still focused on the box in her hand. "I should never have thought that."

Vernon felt like he had been punched in the gut because he knew that he *did* see the world the way she did. Hadn't he been moved by the painting? Hadn't he understood and felt everything she was trying to convey?

But that was the problem.

He couldn't let her know. That would lead to a connection. And, since he and Sadie were so much alike, that connection could blossom into something real. No. He could never let himself draw close to another woman. Not after he failed Lorna so badly. He didn't deserve to love another woman. He couldn't trust himself to protect her.

"Your art is too fancy. Too *Englisch*." Vernon could not believe he was saying the words, even as they left his mouth. His shame magnified as he watched Sadie's expression. The color drained from her face and her features tightened.

"I won't paint in your house again, Vernon. I'm sorry I overstepped." She kept her voice steady, her expression neutral, but Vernon could sense her pain and rejection. He wanted to apologize and explain, but stood silently instead, arms crossed as he watched her hurry out of the kitchen.

It was for the best, he told himself as the door banged shut and he was left alone with his regret.

The next morning, Vernon expected to hear the twins running wild through the house when he followed them back from the morning chores. Surely Sadie would have left at first light. She could easily walk to the phone shanty and organize a ride home. Ned and Newt would be back to their old antics, Lydia would be sad and Arleta would be smug. Vernon's chest felt heavy as he pulled off his muddy work boots, pulled open the screen door and padded into the kitchen in his sock feet.

He was shocked to see Sadie at the stove with a smile on her face, while Lydia stood beside her on a step stool, stirring batter in a mixing bowl. Ned and Newt sat at the table with coloring books. They paused their coloring to elbow one another but seemed surprisingly content. The skillet crackled with hot oil and the smell of bacon filled the air.

"You're still here?" Vernon asked before he could stop himself.

"You think I would abandon *kinner* who need me?" Sadie said without turning to look at him.

Vernon's shame flared inside him. "*Ne.* Of course not. And I'm sorry that I made you feel like you should."

Her lips tightened before she answered. "I'm here to stay until the end of the month. For the *kinner*'s sake."

"*Ya.* I understand. For the *kinner.*" Vernon took off his straw hat and hung it on the peg beside the door. He ran his fingers over his hair as he watched Sadie flip the bacon in the skillet. It took a moment before he could force out the words he knew he had to say. "*Danki.* I'm glad you're here." Then he added hastily, "For the *kinner.*"

Sadie gave a slight nod of acknowledgment. Vernon wished he knew what she was thinking.

"You're going to let it get too crispy," Arleta said from across the room. Vernon's attention shot to where his sister stood in the threshold, halfway in the kitchen, halfway in the hallway that led to the living room.

"I love crispy bacon!" Lydia said.

"*Ya*, but not too crispy," Arleta said. "There's an art to it."

Vernon studied Arleta for a moment. Her body leaned toward the activity on the other side of the kitchen as she stared at the skillet. Her expression was wistful and frustrated.

"Why don't you try?" Vernon suggested gently. "I can tell you want to."

Arleta frowned and waved her hand dismissively.

"I'm serious, Arleta."

"Don't make things harder, Vernon."

"I think you could do okay, if you just try," Vernon said.

"You know I can't follow a recipe anymore," Arleta said. Her face hardened as she spoke, but her eyes stayed on the skillet.

"I know how much you love to cook," Vernon said.

"Loved," Arleta corrected.

"Here." Sadie turned around and held up the spatula in her hand. "Give it a try. No recipe-reading needed."

Arleta frowned.

"*Ach*, go on, Arleta," Vernon said. "What can it hurt?"

"I could get confused about the time and burn the bacon," Arleta said. "Or drop a slice when I flip it. You know how things are now. It won't be as *gut* as I used to make it."

"It will still be *gut* enough."

"Not if I burn it."

"Then we'll start a new batch," Vernon said. "Sadie's right. Give it a try."

"Come on," Ned said.

"We want your bacon again, *Aenti* Arleta," Newt added. "It's the best!"

Arleta hesitated, then shook her head. *"Nee."*

"Why not just give it a try?" Vernon asked gently.

Sadie extended her hand a little farther, silently urging Arleta to cross the room and take the spatula from her.

Arleta shot Vernon a look. "Because I don't want to fail," she said.

"It's *oll recht* to make mistakes," Lydia said as she stirred the batter. She nodded toward a splatter on the counter. "See what I did? I spill a lot when I stir, but Sadie says we all mess up sometimes and not to worry about it."

"I'm too old to make simple mistakes," Arleta shot back.

"No one's too old to make a mistake," Vernon said.

Sadie looked at him for the first time that morning. "That is very true, Vernon," she said as her eyes bored into his. By the intensity of her gaze, he knew that she was trying to tell him that *his* mistakes were okay. Vernon cleared his throat and looked away. "Come on, Arleta," he said to take the attention off of himself.

"Ya!" the three children shouted.

Arleta put her hands on her hips. "Fine, Vernon." She narrowed her eyes. "But only if you try to cook too," she said with a look of triumph.

"Me? Cook?" Vernon laughed and shook his head. "Be sensible, Arleta."

"We want to see *Daed* cook!" Ned shouted.

"Don't be ridiculous," Vernon said. "I work in the fields, not the kitchen. I wouldn't know the first thing about it." As an Amish man, he had never been expected to cook and had never thought to try.

Arleta shrugged. "Then I won't try either."

Vernon's mouth dropped open.

Sadie's lips curled into a half smile. "Not a bad deal, Vernon. If Arleta has to go out of her comfort zone, then so do you."

"Exactly," Arleta said.

"Can you cook me a pie, *Daed*?" Lydia asked.

Sadie chuckled. "Let's start with something simple. Here, Vernon, you can help Lydia with the pancakes."

"Me, make pancakes?"

"*Ya, Daed.* It's easy, see?" Lydia held up the mixing bowl.

"I've done all this all by myself." Lydia glanced up at Sadie. "Well, almost all by myself."

Vernon couldn't help but smile. He threw up his hands. "*Oll recht, oll recht.* I give up." Vernon shook his head as he strode toward the counter, the smile still on his face. "But this means you can't get out of trying too, Arleta."

Arleta's eyes widened. "I never thought you'd actually try to cook, Vernon."

Vernon's smile spread into a grin. "Gotcha, Arleta. Now grab your apron and let's get started."

Soon, the kitchen filled with laughter, the happy smells of cooking and some good-natured teasing. Sadie didn't know what to think. Was this the same man who had stood over her painting the night before, glaring with disapproval? Today, Vernon seemed like a different man. He encouraged Lydia, tousled the twins' hair and even kissed Arleta on the cheek. Arleta swatted him away but couldn't hide her smile.

"Here, Vernon," Sadie said and held out the measuring cup in her hand. "You can cook the next pancake."

"*Ach*, if you say so."

"We say so!" Newt shouted.

Vernon's eyes met Sadie's as he took the cup from her. Their fingers brushed one another's and Sadie felt a jolt. Vernon grinned. Not just his usual, slightly serious half smile, but a real, honest grin. Sadie felt that grin all the way down to her toes. Heat flooded her cheeks and she had to look away. How could Vernon and his family make her feel so good inside? It was almost as if they were all meant to be together.

Sadie pushed the silly thought aside. "Not too much batter," she told Vernon as the cup overflowed. "You'll make a mess."

"So, not the entire cup?"

"*Nee*. Only about half-full or so." Sadie shrugged. "It doesn't really matter, as long as you don't use too much."

"Then why use a cup measure?"

"Stop asking so many questions," Arleta said. "It's just how she does it."

"What about you, Arleta?" Sadie asked.

"I use exactly one third cup for each pancake. I don't estimate like you do."

Sadie had to suppress a smile. "That makes sense."

"Arleta likes to do things just right," Vernon said. "She's very precise."

"Then that's the way we'll do it today," Sadie said. "Lydia, can you grab the third cup measure, please?"

"*Ya!*" Lydia stood on her tiptoes on the stool and reached into the cabinet. She pulled out the third measuring cup, but the quarter measuring cup came tumbling out too. Vernon's arm darted out before Sadie even noticed what was happening and caught the cup, right before it hit her on the head.

"Good catch, *Daed*!" Ned shouted.

Vernon's face lit up. "*Danki, sohn*. You *oll recht*, Sadie?"

"*Ya*, thanks to you." Their eyes locked on to one another for the second time that morning and Sadie felt the familiar rush of emotions again. The sensation flooded her chest and made her heart beat faster.

"We haven't got all day, ain't so?" Arleta interrupted. Sadie's attention shot from Vernon to Arleta and she noticed the knowing look on the woman's face. Sadie felt even warmer—this time with discomfort—and she knew she was blushing. Did Arleta think that she was sweet on Vernon? That would be awkward and embarrassing and completely untrue.

Wouldn't it?

Sadie frowned. "Arleta's right. Vernon has to get to work and we're all getting hungry."

The children all groaned. "But we're having fun," Newt said.

"Don't worry," Sadie said. "We're just getting to the best part. Let's see how well your *daed* can cook a pancake. But first, why don't you show him how, Arleta?"

Arleta hesitated, then scowled and took a step back. "*Ach, nee.* Let's just see what Vernon can do."

"Come on, *Aenti* Arleta!" Ned shouted. "We love your pancakes."

"Well, you used to. I'm not sure…"

Vernon put a gentle hand on Arleta's shoulder. "They don't have to be perfect."

"Humph." Arleta stared at the batter but didn't make a move toward it.

"I'd like to learn from the best," Vernon said.

"I'm not the best anymore."

"Maybe your best is just different now," Vernon said. "I'd still like you to show me."

"*Ach*, fine!" Arleta shook her head in annoyance, but Sadie thought she caught a glimmer of satisfaction pass over her face.

Arleta took the third measuring cup from Lydia, dipped it in the batter, then pulled it out and gave it the perfect little shake to leave the edges free of drips. She poured the batter onto the skillet in a spiral and they all watched as the liquid ran together to form a perfect circle.

"Just like always," Vernon said.

Arleta's face relaxed into what almost looked like a smile.

"I want that pancake!" Lydia said. "It's mine!"

"It's yours," Arleta said.

"Don't you have to flip it?" Vernon asked.

"Just wait," Arleta said. "Just wait…" She picked up the spatula from the spoon rest but didn't move it toward the skillet.

Sadie stepped back to give Arleta more space. This was going better than she had imagined. Maybe Arleta would be able to regain some of her previous skills, eventually. Sadie knew it would be a long, difficult journey, but with enough support, she could see that Arleta could live a more fulfilling life than she had been.

"Now you watch for the bubbles," Arleta said.

"I see a bubble!" Ned shouted.

"Me too!" Newt said.

"But I saw them first!"

"Did not!"

"*Buwe* who argue don't get to pour their own pancakes when it's their turn," Sadie said.

"It's my turn!" Both boys shouted at the same time.

"Let Arleta finish, then it's your *daed*'s turn," Sadie said. "Then you *buwe* will get a chance."

"Now," Arleta said. "When the bubbles look just like this and the edges have that hint of golden brown, that's when you flip it."

Vernon nodded. "Got it."

Arleta's hand faltered and she nearly dropped the spatula. She clenched her jaw in concentration, then slid the spatula underneath the pancake and turned it in one quick movement. The pancake landed with a satisfying slap, the circle perfectly intact.

"If you measure out the batter like I did, your pancake should look exactly like mine," Arleta said to Vernon. "That's the way I like it. Then the pancake stack is even."

Sadie glanced over at the pancakes she had made earlier, before the rest of the family joined in. They were all different sizes, and none of the circles were perfectly round. She had been more focused on chatting with Lydia than on scooping the batter into the skillet.

"But don't they taste the same, whether or not they all look the same?" Newt asked.

"They do," Arleta said as she slid the spatula underneath the pancake and transferred it to the serving platter. "But doesn't it feel *gut* having everything neat and tidy?"

Newt wrinkled his nose. "Not really."

The adults chuckled, especially Sadie, because she understood what Newt meant. She never cared enough to focus on details like making perfectly round pancakes. She would rather daydream.

"*Oll recht*, Vernon." Arleta set the spatula onto the spoon rest and nodded toward the mixing bowl. "Your turn."

"Looks easy," Vernon said. He rolled up his sleeves, picked up the measuring cup and dipped it in the batter. The look of confidence on his face faltered when the batter dripped down the sides of the cup. He tried to imitate Arleta's shake, but batter splattered onto the counter and his blue shirt. "Hey, now. That's not how this is supposed to work."

The children laughed. "You made a mess, *daed*," Lydia said.

"*Ya!*" Newt said. "And you always tell *us* not to make a mess!"

"Humph." Vernon moved the cup toward the skillet. More batter dripped onto the counter. One fat drip fell into the burner and an acrid smell wafted upward. "That's not what I meant to do."

Arleta shook her head, but her eyes were smiling.

Vernon dumped the batter onto the skillet and it formed a misshapen puddle as it sizzled in the oil.

Arleta shook her head again. "You're eating that one, Vernon."

"I believe Newt already pointed out that an ugly pancake tastes just as *gut* as a nice looking one."

"We'll see about that," Arleta said. "You haven't finished cooking it yet."

"You don't think I'm going to burn it do you?"

Arleta's lips curved into a slight smile. "We'll see."

"Why, Arleta," Vernon said in mock seriousness. "It's almost as if you want me to fail. That isn't very nice."

Arleta gave a shrug of exaggerated innocence.

"Are you being naughty, *Aenti* Arleta?" Lydia asked with a serious expression.

The three adults laughed.

"What's so funny?" Lydia asked.

"I'm just joking, Lydia," Arleta said. Then she added, "Mostly," with a sly smile.

Vernon reached for the dishrag beside the sink and began to wipe up the batter he had dripped on the counter and stove. "Just wait, I've got this," he said. He wiped the counter until it shone. "There," he said. "Good as new."

"Vernon, dear?" Arleta asked. "Are you forgetting something?"

Vernon's attention jerked to the stove. *"Ach, nee!"* He lunged for the spatula but only managed to knock it off the spoon rest in his haste. It slid over the edge of the counter and clattered onto the floor. Vernon groaned, bent over and picked it up, then hurried to rinse it off in the sink. Then he shoved the dripping wet spatula under the pancake and flipped it to reveal a blackened underside.

"I thought you weren't going to burn it, Vernon," Arleta said.

Sadie glanced at her and the two women made eye contact. Arleta gave Sadie a wink. Sadie flashed a smile of comradery. It was the second time the two of them had connected over something funny. Sadie felt hope swell within her. This morning had gone better than she ever could have imagined, burnt pancake and all.

Chapter Nine

Vernon felt energized for the rest of the day. The sun shone brighter and the sky looked bluer. Even Big Red seemed easier to work with. Vernon was behind schedule with the farm work after spending that time in the kitchen, but it had been more than worth it. The twins hadn't caused any trouble and Arleta had actually seemed to enjoy herself for the first time since the accident. Now the boys were helping to bring in the hay without any complaints.

A warm bubble of hope formed deep inside his chest. Maybe, just maybe, his family was on the road to recovery. For the first time, he thought he could see a light at the end of a dark, difficult path.

None of this would have happened without Sadie. Somehow, she had brought joy and healing into their lives. He didn't quite know how she had done it. In fact, some people might say that Sadie was the last person they would expect to bring such a positive change. She was a likable young woman for certain sure, but there had always been whispers about her throughout the church district. It wasn't quite right for a good Amish woman to be so creative. People complained that it put too much attention on her and could lead to pride. Or, that it simply wasn't the way things were done. Among the Amish, there were certain ways of doing things, and any other way was met with suspicion.

"This is too fancy," Arleta had said after seeing Sadie's paintings for sale in Aunt Fannie's Amish Gifts a few months back. "That sort of thing is for the *Englisch*, not for us." Arleta's opinion was echoed by many. But Vernon had always been fascinated by Sadie's paintings. The last time he had been in the gift shop he had stared at a scene that she had painted of a fiery red sunset over a glistening lake. The image had made him feel a longing inside that he couldn't quite name. He wished he could buy the painting, but he knew Arleta would never approve. Besides, that sort of decoration was for *Englisch* tourists' homes, not Amish ones.

But ever since then, Vernon always thought of Sadie's painting when he watched the sunset over the west pasture in an orange glow that shimmered over the rows of wheat.

Vernon sent the boys in from the fields at their bedtime. He came in later that evening, his back aching and a new blister forming on his left hand. But he felt satisfied with his work and didn't mind that he had had to make up for the time he had lost that morning. It had been worth it. He would work all night if it meant he could see Arleta give a genuine smile again.

Big Red tugged hard on the lead as they neared the barn. He was ready for his oats. "*Oll recht*, big *bu*, we'll get your dinner, *ya*?" Vernon gave the draft horse a firm pat on his muscled shoulder, then frowned as they neared the weathered building. "Looks like we've got company." Vernon studied the light that flickered through the barn window and wondered who had lit a kerosene lantern. He hoped the twins weren't hiding in the hayloft again.

Vernon pushed open the heavy double door as Big Red led the way toward his stall, heavy hoofs clomping rhythmically on the floor and echoing against the high ceiling. "Anyone there?" Vernon asked the empty space. There was no answer except for a restless whinny from Old Max. "I'll get you some oats too, *ya*?" Vernon glanced around and realized the light was coming from the tack room, where he stored extra supplies and did his bookkeeping. "Hello?" he asked, louder this time.

When they reached his stall, Big Red whinnied, then pushed against Vernon's chest with his muzzle, shoving him back a step. "You don't know your own strength, *bu*. Easy now. I'll get your oats." Vernon hurried to remove Big Red's halter, then poured a generous serving of oats into his feed bucket. "I'll be back in a minute to give you a rubdown. Just let me see who's in the tack room. I hope those *buwe* of mine aren't up to no *gut*." Big Red shoved his muzzle into the bucket of oats and ignored Vernon as he strode away.

Vernon paused when he reached the doorway of the tack room. Sadie stood in front of an easel, her back to the door. The brush in her hand flew over a canvas, creating splashing swirls of color that reminded Vernon of ripples in a lake during the summertime. He stared, fascinated, as the brushstrokes sharpened to create a clearer image before his eyes. The sparkling, sunlit water brought up a strange surge of emotion, and he knew that if he allowed himself to feel that emotion, everything else he had forced down over the last year would come bubbling to the surface. He couldn't let Sadie bring those emotions out of him. There was a reason he had fought so hard to suppress them all.

"What are you doing?" Vernon asked. His voice sounded harsher than he meant it to.

Sadie jumped and spun around. "I didn't know you were there. Sometimes I get so caught up…" She cleared her throat and set down her brush. "The *kinner* are all asleep. They had a *gut* time with you this morning. It was all they talked about at bedtime."

"Ya." Vernon frowned. He wanted to thank Sadie for helping him connect with his children again, but he was too afraid of what he was feeling inside. "I told you not to paint in my house."

A flicker of vulnerability passed over Sadie's face. Then she lifted her chin and said, "But this isn't your house. It's the barn."

Vernon grunted. There was a tense moment, then he shook his head and chuckled. "You got me there."

Sadie exhaled and Vernon could see the tension leave her shoulders. They stared at each other until Vernon looked away. He rubbed the back of his neck with his hand. "What, uh, what are you painting?"

Sadie looked surprised at the question. "That lake past the Yoder farm where people like to swim. The one with the sunflower field beside it."

"Ya. I know the one."

Vernon squinted at the image on the canvas. "But it doesn't look quite like that lake, ain't so?"

Sadie's lips curled into a soft smile. *"Nee.* That's kind of the point."

Vernon frowned and squinted at the painting. "Ah. *Oll recht."* He studied the vague outline of yellow sunflowers waving in a warm summer breeze. Of course the painting couldn't *show* warmth, but he sensed it was summer and he sensed it was warm. He wondered how Sadie could convey that from a few blobs and swirls of color. "I've never seen anything like your paintings before," Vernon said.

Sadie's expression became more guarded. *"Nee.* Not many people in Bluebird Hills understand what I do. It was an unexpected blessing when Katie started selling my art in her gift shop."

Vernon ran his fingers through his beard as he studied the painting. "The *Englisch* understand, ain't so?"

"They buy my paintings, so I guess some of them do."

Vernon grunted.

Another awkward moment passed. Sadie frowned and began to gather up her tubes of paint. "I'm sorry. I'll get this all put away. I know you don't like it."

"I never said I didn't like it."

Sadie's eyes shot to him. "But…"

Vernon shrugged. "Maybe I even understand it, a little."

"You do?"

"Maybe. But I could be wrong about what I see in this painting."

Sadie's face lit up. "*Nee*. It's up to you. There's no right or wrong way to see it."

Vernon chuckled. "I'm not sure that makes sense. But I like the idea."

Sadie's gaze stayed on him as he spoke. Vernon sensed she could see through him, to what was hidden inside. For the first time, instead of wanting to shut her out, he felt that being seen could be a huge relief. What if he laid down the burden he carried, stopped hiding and just let everything out? Would the world really stop turning?

"Maybe we have something in common," Sadie murmured.

Vernon frowned. "What's that?"

Sadie bit her lip and looked away. She picked up her paintbrush and dipped it in the Mason jar to clean it.

"What do we have in common?" Vernon urged softly. He could feel the connection forming between them, but it was as fragile as a soap bubble. He didn't want it to burst, but he had to know what she was thinking.

Sadie kept her attention on the paintbrush. "Maybe you

don't always feel that you belong in Bluebird Hills either," Sadie said softly.

She looked so vulnerable all of a sudden that Vernon wanted to scoop her up and hold her. "Maybe." He didn't want to say more, but he could see she needed the reassurance. "Maybe I've thought about leaving," Vernon added. "Maybe sometimes I just want to go where nobody knows me…or what I've done."

"And maybe, sometimes, I want to go where people don't think that there's something wrong with me for wanting to capture what I feel on canvas."

Silence took over the room as they both considered the other's admission. The only sound was a snort from Old Max and a chomping noise as Big Red ate his oats in the other room. "Will you leave?" Vernon finally asked. He was surprised to feel his chest constrict at the thought of what she might say.

Sadie shook her head. "*Nee.* This is home. And I believe in living a Plain life. I would never jump the fence. It's just that the rest of the church district doesn't always agree with me about what's Plain and what's fancy."

"I think you have more support than you realize," Vernon said. "You have a *gut* heart. Everyone sees that. It's just that no one else around here is quite like you. People don't know what to make of that. I think it scares them a little."

"Why should it scare them?" Sadie asked.

"I don't know. Because people are afraid of what they don't understand, I guess. Because they don't know where you fit into their idea of how things should be."

"I'm so careful, Vernon. I work extra hard—harder than my friends—to do everything just right to make up for being different. I always measure the length of my dresses and the folds on my *kapp* with a ruler. I never push the boundaries on what colors or fabrics to use in my clothing. I follow the rules. I really do. I don't sign my paintings, so I'm not drawing attention to myself. And I never paint people. I'm careful about that. I don't want to disappoint *Gott* by making a graven image."

Vernon took a step closer. His heart pounded in his throat as he neared her. She looked so fragile, so in need of reassurance. All she wanted was to be seen, to be understood. He knew how that felt. Somehow, his hand moved to her arm. He had not meant to let that happen. But, instead of flinching or pulling away, she relaxed beneath his touch. "I know, Sadie. No one can fault you, that's for certain sure."

"But they do. What I don't understand is, why would *Gott* give me the talent if he didn't want me to use it?"

"I don't know." Vernon hesitated, then shrugged. "The only answer that makes sense to me is that *Gott* does want you to use it."

Sadie nodded. She opened her mouth, then closed it again.

"What?" Vernon asked.

"Nothing." Sadie broke eye contact and looked down at the paintbrush in her hand.

"You were going to say something."

Sadie took a deep breath. "I have an idea, but I don't know if you'll like it. Maybe I shouldn't bring it up."

"It's *oll recht*. You can tell me." Vernon smiled. "So what if I don't like it? We can have a difference of opinion, *ya*?"

Sadie's expression eased and she chuckled. "Now who sounds different from other people? Not many people welcome a difference of opinion, especially from an employee."

The word *employee* struck Vernon. He had almost forgotten that was why Sadie was here. The flickering kerosene light, the earthy warmth of the barn, the genuine need for understanding in her eyes—it had taken Vernon somewhere else for a moment. He had been talking to a friend, not an employee. Perhaps, if he admitted it, someone whom he wanted to be more than a friend.

"I welcome your opinion, Sadie," he said simply.

Sadie smiled. "*Oll recht.* I'd like to try to help Arleta. The *Englisch* use art to help people recover from trauma. They call it art therapy. I've heard it can help people with head injuries." Sadie twisted the paintbrush between her fingers. Vernon gave her a nod of encouragement. "Maybe this is a way that *Gott* can use my talent for *gut.* I know I'm not an art therapist—you have to have an advanced degree for that. But maybe I can still be of some help. I've read a lot of books about it and I even took a class on it in Lancaster last year, on my *Rumspringa.* I've had this idea for a long time. I just didn't know who *Gott* wanted me to help until I came here."

Vernon felt a wave of relief sweep through him. He knew Sadie had been a blessing for his family already, but could God have sent Sadie to do even more? "*Ya.* I like that idea."

"You do?"

Vernon chuckled. "Don't look so surprised."

"I wasn't sure…"

"Because I'm a grumpy old recluse who would never accept something new or different?"

Sadie blushed. "Something like that."

"Maybe there's more to me than you realize." Had he really just said that? What was he trying to prove? He felt an uncomfortable catch in his throat. This conversation was getting too personal—and worst of all, he wanted it to.

Sadie's mouth parted as if to ask a question, but she said nothing. She just stared into his eyes.

Vernon cleared his throat and looked away. "I'll, uh, talk to Arleta. She won't like it, but I'll convince her."

"Can you do that?"

Vernon flashed a sly grin. "I can try."

Chapter Ten

The next morning, Sadie woke up feeling excited about the day. She could hardly believe how she and Vernon had connected the night before. The memory felt like a warm hug.

Arleta was in her glider chair, as usual, when Sadie emerged from her bedroom, dressed in a freshly starched *kapp* and sapphire blue cape dress. The green blinds were partially raised, allowing a thin ray of early morning sun into the living room. Dust motes danced in the yellow light as Arleta glided slowly and rhythmically. Her hands moved restlessly across her lap. The room was still somewhat dim, but Sadie was struck by the difference just a little bit of light made.

"Gude Mariye," Sadie said. "It's nice in here this morning."

Arleta grunted.

"Would you like to *kumme* help with breakfast again this morning? Yesterday was fun."

Arleta hesitated. *"Nee.* I'm tired. But maybe another day."

"Oll recht."

"Anyway, Vernon's got something up his sleeve, so I better save my energy."

"You talked to Vernon this morning?" Sadie instinctively glanced toward the window. The yard was empty. Only a rooster strutted in the dirt beneath the big oak tree. Purple clouds bruised the sky behind the rising sun and the distant cornfield sparkled with dew.

"*Ya*. You just missed him. He came to tell me that he's taking us out when he comes in from the fields today."

Sadie's heart skipped a beat. She tried not to smile. She didn't want Arleta to know, but she liked the idea of going out with Vernon. "Oh. Did he say where?"

"*Nee*, but I wasn't born yesterday. I know what's going on."

"What?" Sadie froze. Did Arleta suspect that Sadie and Vernon had formed a connection? It had all happened so fast that Sadie still wasn't sure it was real. How could Arleta know?

"He's trying to butter me up, obviously. Vernon never goes out. So he must want something." The tension left Sadie's body. Arleta didn't suspect anything—anything about Sadie and Vernon, anyway. "*Ach*, well, you may as well have fun, whether or not he wants something."

"Humph. Vernon knows I don't like to go out. I might refuse."

"I'm sure he's planning on going somewhere you'll like. Someplace without a lot of people and noise."

Arleta sighed. "I suppose."

Sadie softened her voice. "I'm sure he means well, Arleta. He cares about you."

Arleta's eyebrows snapped down. "I don't need you to tell me how my own *bruder* feels about me."

Sadie flinched. "Right. Of course. I'm going to go make breakfast before the *kinner* wake up." And then she fled the *dawdi haus* and Arleta's judgmental stare.

Sadie found a note on the kitchen table as soon as she walked into the farmhouse.

Don't cook supper tonight. I have a plan.
—Vernon

Sadie reread the note twice before setting it back down. She was distracted for the rest of the day. She barely noticed the twins' antics or Arleta's disapproving scowl. All she could think about was spending time with Vernon that evening. The thought gave her heart an extra beat and made her toes tingle. She told herself that she was being silly, but she couldn't help feeling *something* after last night. Vernon had understood her—really understood her. He was the first person who had ever made her feel seen and heard. And now, she couldn't shake it.

The sun finally made its way down its slow, daily arc, and Sadie saw Vernon and the twins coming in from the fields. "Your *daed*'s coming home!" she said to Lydia. "Hurry and get your shoes on. Then run and tell *Aenti* Arleta it's time to go."

"Do we have to wear shoes?" Lydia asked. "We never do."

"Not at home in the summer, but you need them to go out. Especially since we don't know where we're going."

"*Oll recht*. I like surprises!" Lydia said as she raced upstairs to grab her black athletic shoes.

"And don't forget your socks!" Sadie shouted up the stairwell.

Everyone was lined up in the yard before Vernon finished hitching up Old Max to the buggy. Even Arleta seemed excited at the prospect of a surprise outing, despite her protests. Vernon caught Sadie's eye as he buckled the last strap on the leather harness. He winked and Sadie's chest leaped into her throat. She and Vernon had definitely formed a connection last night. Now they had a plan to help Arleta and it made Sadie feel special to have a secret between the two of them.

The children bounced in the back seat of the buggy the entire way. Once, Ned dropped his straw hat over the side and Vernon had to stop the buggy, circle back and collect it before a blue pickup truck ran it over.

"That was a close call," Lydia said. "I'm glad my *kapp* is pinned on."

"Ned wouldn't lose his hat if he didn't dangle it out of the buggy," Arleta said in a firm voice, but her eyes were smiling. "He likes trouble. Just like his *daed* at that age."

"My *daed* used to get into trouble?" Lydia asked. Her mouth hung open in surprise.

"Oh, *ya*," Arleta said. "He was a real *schnickelfritz*, for certain sure."

Vernon and Sadie exchanged a smile from their seats in the front of the buggy. "Is that true, Vernon?" Sadie asked with a twinkle in her eye. "Were you a troublemaker?"

Vernon gave an innocent shrug.

"What did you do to get in trouble, *Daed*?" Newt shouted from the back seat of the buggy.

"*Ach*, well, I'd tell you, but there's no time." He nodded up the road, while keeping both hands on the reins. "We're here."

"You just don't want to give us any ideas, *Daed*," Ned said.

"For sure and certain," Arleta said. Sadie and Vernon laughed, and Arleta joined in. Then she craned her head from the back seat to see where they were headed. "That's my favorite restaurant."

"*Ya.*" Vernon grinned and guided Old Max to the right, toward a building that looked like it belonged in an old-fashioned German village. The cheerful yellow walls were crisscrossed with wooden beams. Each window was lined with green shutters and window boxes filled with pink tulips. A wooden windmill stood beside the parking lot, its big green blades turning slowly in the hot summer breeze.

A hand-painted sign beneath the windmill depicted a horse and buggy and the words The Old Amish Kitchen.

"Did you paint the sign?" Vernon asked as he tugged the reins and the buggy shuddered to a stop.

"I did." Sadie tried not to feel pride, but she was tempted when she saw how Vernon was admiring her work.

"It's very *gut*," he said as he stared up at the sign.

"Vernon, you know I don't like going inside crowded places," Arleta cut in. "Look at all the cars and buggies in the parking lot. It's too much. I'm not going in." Her face crumpled with disappointment. "I don't know why you brought me here."

Vernon pulled the hand brake and swiveled in his seat. "You're not going in."

"Then why are we here?" Arleta asked.

"I told you, I have a plan. Just wait in the buggy."

Arleta frowned, then leaned back in the bench seat without saying anything else.

"Can we come, *Daed*?" Newt asked.

"I'll be back before you can say jackrabbit," Vernon said. "Keep *Aenti* Arleta and Sadie company while I'm gone."

Vernon handed the reins to Sadie to hold and hopped out of the buggy. The boys both shouted "jackrabbit" as soon as his feet hit the ground.

"You lied!" Ned said.

"It's a figure of speech," Vernon shouted as he hurried across the parking lot, before either of his sons could get another word in.

Vernon reappeared a couple of minutes later with a brown paper bag in each hand. He held them up and smiled as he walked toward the buggy. "Dinner to go."

"That *was* fast," Lydia said as Vernon handed the bags to Sadie and climbed into his seat. "I called the restaurant from the phone shanty this morning and ordered ahead. They had everything ready." He released the hand brake, took the reins back from Sadie and clicked his tongue. "Let's go, Old Max." The buggy lurched into motion.

Lydia bounced up and down in her seat. "Where are we going to eat?" she asked.

Vernon just smiled.

The buggy wound its way down narrow country lanes surrounded by rolling hills and pastureland. Rambling farmhouses, red barns and white silos dotted the hillsides. Vernon turned onto a dirt road and they bumped along the washboard surface until the road dead-ended at a sharp embankment covered in wildflowers. At the bottom of the embankment, the still, blue waters of a lake shone in the late afternoon sun. A field of bright orange sunflowers spread across the far bank, with the Yoder farmhouse and barn standing in the distance. The Yoders owned the lake, but they wanted to share their blessing with the community and everyone in the church district had an open invitation to enjoy the swimming hole. Summer evenings often drew a handful of families.

Sadie looked at Vernon. "This is the lake I was painting last night."

Vernon looked sheepish. *"Ya."*

Sadie didn't know what to say. It made her feel special that Vernon wanted to bring her here, in person.

"You captured it perfectly, you know."

They were interrupted by a tumble of small bodies as the children climbed over the seats and toppled out the buggy doors.

"Let's go!" Newt shouted.

"Look! Simon's here!" Ned yelled as he pointed to another buggy parked alongside the dirt road.

"And Priss!" Lydia added as she pointed to a second buggy.

"Don't go near the water until I get there," Vernon shouted to his children, then looked over his shoulder to Arleta, who was still sitting in the back seat. "Is it *oll recht* that the Millers and Kings are here? I thought we might have the place to ourselves, since we got here early and it's a weekday."

Arleta hesitated. "I think it will be *oll recht*. Being outside is easier than being inside someone's home. There's more space for the noise to go, if that makes sense. It doesn't feel as overwhelming."

"It does make sense," Sadie said.

"But after we left the Millers' in such a hurry last time..." Arleta's mouth tightened and she looked down. "I'm not sure how to face them."

Vernon swallowed and Sadie could see the concern on his face as well. She wished she could take the embarrassment from him. Especially now that she knew what he had been thinking and feeling last Sunday when he fled the Millers' house. "I think the best way is to remember that they're our friends," Sadie said. "That means they still love us when we're not at our best, ain't so?"

Arleta didn't reply, but her expression showed that she was considering Sadie's words.

Vernon nodded. "For certain sure." He jumped from the buggy and tied Old Max's lead to a tree trunk before jogging around the buggy to offer Sadie a hand down. She liked the feel of his warm, strong hand in hers as she slid to the ground. He made sure she had her balance before letting go and opening Arleta's door. "Let me help you."

"I don't need help," she said and waved him away.

Vernon grinned. "Ah, now that's the Arleta I know."

Arleta rolled her eyes. "Let's eat. I'm starving."

Vernon leaned into the buggy and pulled out a red-and-white-checkered blanket from behind the bench seat. "I brought a picnic blanket."

"Perfect," Sadie said as she grabbed the paper bags from The Old Amish Kitchen.

Arleta hesitated when they crested the embankment and saw Katie and Levi Miller sitting on a log alongside Gabriel and Eliza King. Levi's son, Simon, stood at the edge of the water holding a turtle, while the Kings' foster daughter, Priss, waded in the shallows. Ned and Newt were already at Simon's side, jostling to see the turtle. Lydia hung back near the adults, looking a little concerned about getting too close to the reptile.

When the Kings and Millers saw the trio they all smiled and waved.

"Hello!" Katie said. "What a fun surprise to run into you all here. The *kinner* are already having a *gut* time together. We should do this more often."

Sadie felt a wave of relief over the warm welcome. Good friends were worth their weight in gold.

"Come join us," Levi said and patted the log. "There's plenty of room."

"I brought a blanket to sit on," Eliza said. "To keep my dress from getting snagged on the wood. Arleta, *kumme* sit by me and we can share." Eliza was always careful to keep things neat and tidy. In fact, it was unusual to see her foster daughter, Priss, splashing in muddy water.

"Looks like Priss is having fun," Sadie said as she neared the log.

"Ya." Eliza scooted closer to Gabriel to make room for Arleta. "Priss gets into all kinds of messes these days. Yesterday, she made mud pies in the backyard. I have to admit

he's been a *gut* influence." She nudged her husband in the side with her elbow. "Ain't so, Gabriel?"

Gabriel looked at his wife with love in his eyes. "Not as *gut* an influence as you've been on me."

Sadie felt a pang of envy as she witnessed the connection between the newlyweds. Eliza and Gabriel were complete opposites, so no one had ever guessed they would end up together. But as soon as they started walking out together— to everyone's surprise—they were a perfect match. Sadie wondered what it would feel like to settle down with someone who truly knew and understood her, and even appreciated her quirks.

She wanted what Gabriel and Eliza had.

Sadie caught herself glancing at Vernon. Hadn't he made her feel understood when they talked about her painting last night in the barn? Who else had ever appreciated her talent in the way he had? Sure, Katie Miller encouraged Sadie to sell her art in the Millers' gift shop, but Katie had never connected with Sadie over her art quite like Vernon had. Katie appreciated Sadie's art from a business standpoint. With Vernon, it was different. He saw what was behind the art. Talking to him about that made her feel like there were little fireworks zipping through her veins.

And now, he had brought her to the lake she had painted. He was communicating that he appreciated her art through actions and not just words.

"You *oll recht*?" Vernon asked Arleta in a low voice. His hand was on her arm to keep her steady as they navigated the uneven ground.

"Ya," she whispered. "Of course. Don't make a scene."

Vernon gave a solemn nod, but kept his hand on her arm until she was safely seated on the log.

"How's your wheat looking this year?" Levi asked as

Sadie and Vernon settled onto the rough, makeshift seat. Sadie wanted to thank Levi for bringing up casual conversation to put them all at ease. Maybe Arleta and Vernon could relax now.

"*Gut,*" Vernon nodded. "It's looking *gut*. A fine crop."

"Same for us," Levi said. "*Gott* has blessed us this year."

They chatted for a while as they watched the children splash and play by the water. Then Vernon spread out the big picnic blanket, called the children over and offered to share the food from the Old Amish Kitchen with the other families. The Millers and Kings added the food they had brought to the spread and they all ate an unexpected potluck dinner together.

Sadie noticed that Arleta kept to the edge of the group, but she sat with them through supper without any conflict. Her eyes stayed on the scenery around them most of the time, and Sadie sensed that being in nature soothed Arleta. Even so, Sadie felt a huge relief when they all said their goodbyes for the evening. She was thankful everything had gone so well.

After the Kings and Millers left, Vernon immediately turned to Arleta. "How are you holding up? Did you get one of your headaches?"

"*Nee.* I'm *oll recht.* The *kinner* had plenty of room to play, so it wasn't too loud near me. And there weren't a lot of people talking at once, so I could follow the conversation without feeling overloaded. It was nice being here." She took a deep breath and let it out slowly. It was the first time that Sadie had seen Arleta seem relaxed. "I've always liked this place. It's peaceful." Orange rays of low evening sun danced across the surface of the lake. Crickets hummed in the tall grass and a handful of lighting bugs flashed their lights above the water.

"I know," Vernon said and grinned.

Arleta turned to Vernon and raised an eyebrow. "So. You got my favorite food and brought me to one of my favorite places. What do you want from me?"

"Hey, it's one of Sadie's favorite places too."

"Is it?"

"Ya," Sadie said. She and Vernon made eye contact and Sadie felt an understanding pass between them. Warmth filled her chest.

"Me too!" Lydia piped up from where she sat on the ground nearby, wrapped in a big towel with her knees pulled up to her chin. "I love swimming with Priss. We all love it here, *Aenti* Arleta."

"Nonetheless, I know when you're trying to butter me up, Vernon Kauffman." Arleta's hands moved to her hips.

"Oll recht, oll recht. We—Sadie and I—have an idea." Vernon rubbed the back of his neck.

"But you're scared to tell me what it is."

Vernon gave a sheepish shrug. "Maybe."

Arleta rolled her eyes. "Spit it out, Vernon. I won't bite."

"How would you like to capture all this beauty?" Vernon nodded toward the lake. The sky had turned purple above the distant fields and the first star twinkled on the horizon.

"Ach, you know Amish don't take photographs."

"Nee, but how about painting it?"

"Don't be absurd, Vernon."

"I'm serious, Arleta."

"Then don't admit that you're serious. It's not right."

"Why not? As long as you're not creating a graven image then what could be wrong with it? The bishop and the elders allow Sadie to paint. You could try it too."

"Vernon, the very idea. Why would I want to do a thing like that, anyway?"

"It might help," Sadie cut in. Her voice faltered and she tried to sound more confident than she felt. "There's something called art therapy. It's used to help people with injuries like yours to rehabilitate."

"Ned and Newt, don't go back in the water!" Vernon shouted. The two boys froze where they had crept back to the edge of the lake. "*Kumme* over here and dry off. We're leaving in five minutes." Vernon gave them an I-mean-business look, then turned his attention back to Sadie and Arleta. "Sorry, Sadie. Go on."

"Nee." Arleta shook her head. "Don't bother. I don't want to hear it. Painting is fancy. It's for *Englischers*, not Amish. And this isn't any of your business, anyway, Sadie. You don't have a right to meddle like this."

Sadie's cheeks burned. She felt exposed, as if she had been caught doing something shameful, even though she knew that she wasn't doing anything wrong. "I'm sorry. But I had to try to help. I can't just stand by…" Sadie struggled to put her thoughts into words under Arleta's hard stare. "Have you been to rehabilitation therapy at all, Arleta? You need help getting better."

"I tried and it didn't work, so I quit. Not that it's any of your business."

"But it takes time. You can't just quit."

"What do you know about it?" Arleta asked. "You're not a doctor."

"Nee. Of course not. But I've learned how important rehabilitation therapy is for people with traumatic brain injuries. Not just art therapy, but occupational therapy, physical therapy, speech therapy and more."

"I don't need any of that. I told you, I tried and it didn't work."

"You didn't try long enough," Vernon said gently.

"I didn't like it, Vernon. You know that. It made me feel weak. All it did was show how much I couldn't do anymore."

"I'm sorry," Vernon said. His face hardened. "I wish I could fix it for you. I wish it had been me instead."

"Stop that, Vernon." Arleta frowned at her brother. "I won't let you talk like that."

Vernon stared at Arleta.

"Anyway, we're Amish." Arleta shook her head. "We don't need worldly *Englisch* help."

"Getting *gut* medical care isn't worldly, Arleta. It's the right thing to do, whether you're *Englisch* or Amish."

"If you don't want to go to *Englisch* therapy, you could start at home with some art therapy," Sadie said. "That might feel less intimidating and less worldly."

Arleta rubbed her temples. "I already said *nee*. It won't help and it's too fancy. Now take me home, Vernon. All this stress has given me one of my headaches."

Vernon managed to mouth the words "I'm sorry" to Sadie as they bundled the children into the buggy, but that couldn't alleviate the heaviness she felt in her heart. How could she help Arleta, if Arleta refused to be helped? All Sadie could do was turn her attention to someone she *could* help. That gave her an idea.

Sadie tucked a dry towel around Lydia, shut the back door of the buggy and jogged around front, to where Vernon was untying Old Max's lead from the tree trunk. "Vernon." Sadie kept her voice low and glanced into the buggy to see if Arleta was listening. "Would you let the *kinner* try art therapy? It can help with mental health too. And it might win Arleta over if she sees it help the *kinner*."

Vernon furrowed his brow. "Mental health? My *kinner* are fine. They don't have those kinds of problems."

Sadie put a hand on Vernon's sleeve. "They've been

through a lot, losing their *mamm*. It could help them cope with the loss. Struggling with mental health isn't something to be ashamed of. It happens to everyone at some point in their lives, especially when they've suffered a loss."

Vernon kept his eyes on the lead. His fingers fumbled over the leather and Sadie knew her words had thrown him. "I'm sorry I brought it up, Vernon. I didn't mean to overstep." Sadie bit her lip. She was always too pushy when she felt passionate about something.

Vernon fumbled with the lead for another moment, then stopped and exhaled. "*Nee.* You're just trying to help." His eyes flicked up to hers. "If you think it will help them, then go ahead." He lowered his voice to a whisper. "It's hard to admit that they might need help. People say *kinner* are resilient, but…"

"But they need a lot of love and care to make them resilient," Sadie finished for him.

"*Ya.*" Vernon gave a serious nod. "That's right."

"Pretending that we don't need help doesn't make the problem go away," Sadie said gently. Her heart pounded against her breastbone as she hoped that she hadn't said too much.

But Vernon just gave a wry half smile. "Tell that to Arleta."

They both laughed and Sadie knew she and Vernon had joined forces in a way she could never have imagined the day she had arrived at the Kauffman farm.

Chapter Eleven

Sadie couldn't wait to start teaching the Kauffman children to paint. She rushed through her chores the next morning and, as soon as the last breakfast dish was washed, dried and put away, she gathered them all in the barn. She still couldn't quite believe that Vernon had given his blessing for this. Sadie hoped that he would be impressed when he came in from the fields that evening. As for Arleta, well, Sadie hoped she wouldn't notice what they were doing. Sadie knew she wouldn't approve. She might even try to convince Vernon to stop letting the children paint.

Sadie set up an old card table in the middle of the tack room and laid out all the supplies.

"Is this going to be messy?" Newt asked as Sadie fastened a big black garbage bag around him as a makeshift apron.

"Maybe," Sadie said as she used duct tape to fasten the bag together in the back.

"Yay!" Newt pumped a fist in the air. "I love messy."

"*Gut*. Because now you can make a mess and it doesn't matter. All the paint will go on the garbage bag instead of your clothes."

"Is that why we're painting in the barn?" Ned asked.

"*Ya.*"

"What are we supposed to paint?" Lydia asked as Sadie passed out the paintbrushes.

"I'm not going to tell you what to paint."

"You're not?" Newt crinkled up his nose in surprise. *"Nee."*

"But our teacher at school always tells us what to do."

"This isn't school," Sadie said as she sat down in a folding chair beside Lydia. "And I'm not a teacher. There are people who go to school for a long time to learn how to help children through art, but I stopped school after eighth grade, of course. But I do know that painting can be *gut* for you. So this is just a fun thing for us to do together. And maybe, hopefully, it will help you feel better."

"How can painting make us feel better?" Ned looked skeptical. "Anyway, I'm not sick."

"I mean that it might help you feel better emotionally. Do you ever feel sad or angry and you're not sure how to handle the feeling?"

Ned paused, then shrugged. "Maybe."

"Sometimes I feel sad because I miss *Mamm*," Lydia murmured as she turned her big, brown eyes to Sadie.

Sadie squeezed Lydia's hand. "Let's all close our eyes for a moment and check in about how we feel right now."

"That sounds silly," Newt said.

"I don't get it," Ned said.

"Um, just close your eyes and notice what you feel inside," Sadie said.

"If you say so," Ned grumbled.

Sadie waited a few beats. "Okay. Now put that feeling on the paper."

"Huh?" Newt crinkled his nose again.

"Just paint whatever comes naturally. It doesn't have to be anything in particular. It doesn't have to look like anything. It can just be colors. Or it can be something specific in real life that you're thinking about. There's no right or wrong. Just paint!"

"Isn't there always a right and wrong way to do things?" Ned asked. He dipped his brush into the red paint, then held up the brush as he stared at the blank canvas paper in front of him.

That was a complicated question. "Oftentimes, yes," Sadie answered carefully, "but when it comes to art and expressing how we feel deep down, there's no right or wrong. You can paint a house or an ocean or a rock—it doesn't matter. It's whatever feels right to you."

"Got it," Ned murmured, then began to paint.

Sadie smiled. This just might work. Soon, all four of them were painting. The still, humid air was punctuated by the sound of bristles whispering across canvas paper. In the background, Old Max whinnied and snorted. A fly buzzed somewhere near the ceiling. It was the first time Sadie had ever witnessed the twins sitting in complete silence for so long. They didn't even fidget.

Sadie didn't know how much time had passed when Ned finally slammed down his brush and shouted, "Done!"

"Can I see?" Sadie asked.

"Ya."

Ned turned the canvas paper around so Sadie could view it right side up. *"Wunderbar,"* Sadie said as she studied the red and gray swirls that formed a funnel-shaped spiral. "Would you like to tell me about your painting?"

"Ummm…" Ned glanced at Newt, who was slouched over his own painting, his tongue sticking out in concentration. Ned shrugged. *"Oll recht.* I guess so."

Lydia looked up from her painting to dip her brush in the water jar. "Ohhh, I like that, Ned."

Ned beamed. "It's a tornado."

"A red tornado?" Lydia asked.

"*Ya.* Sadie said we could paint stuff the way we wanted."

Sadie gave an encouraging nod. "That's right. What made you choose red, Ned?"

Ned bit his lip.

"You don't have to share," Sadie said. "It's up to you. But sometimes it makes people feel better to explain how they feel."

Ned shifted in his seat. "I made it red because that's the color I feel a lot."

"How can you feel a color?" Lydia asked.

"I don't know. You just can. I was thinking about how I felt and this is what I saw."

"*Gut*, Ned. That makes sense to me. And Lydia, it's *oll recht* if it doesn't make sense to you. We're all different."

"Sometimes I feel like a tornado ripped through my life," Ned said.

Newt's eyes jumped from his painting to his brother's and he straightened in his chair. Sadie suspected he could relate to what Ned was saying. She held her breath, hoping that nothing stopped Ned from continuing.

"I feel real mad sometimes." Ned motioned toward his painting. "That's why the tornado is red. Sometimes I even feel like I've turned into a tornado because I get so mad that I want to rip stuff apart, just like a tornado."

"That sounds like a lot of emotions for a boy to handle," Sadie said.

Ned shrugged. "I didn't used to feel that way."

"Our *mamm* died," Newt cut in. Ned and Lydia nodded. "It makes me mad too," he added.

"And it makes me sad," Lydia said.

"It isn't fair," Ned said.

"*Nee,*" Sadie responded gently. "It's not."

"I don't understand why it happened," Newt said. "Or why *Aenti* Arleta isn't like she used to be."

Sadie let out a long, slow breath as she said a quick silent prayer for guidance. "No one can understand why *gut* people pass away or get hurt. It's a mystery that only *Gott* can understand. But you know what else is a mystery of *Gott*?"

"What?" Ned and Newt asked in unison.

"How much He loves us—we can't even imagine how much. And how He stays with us through all the bad things that happen, no matter what. That's how we can get through them."

The children sat in silence for a moment as they took in Sadie's words. "Do you think things will be okay?" Ned asked finally.

"*Ya*. I know they will. You'll never stop missing your *mamm*, but *Gott* always has a *gut* plan for redemption."

"What does redemption mean?" Lydia asked.

Sadie wondered how to explain the concept simply. She rolled her paintbrush between her thumb and finger as she thought about it. "It's when *Gott* turns something bad into something *gut*."

"That's a *gut* way of explaining it," a deep voice said from behind Sadie. She smiled and turned to see Vernon leaning against the door jamb, a look of appreciation on his face.

"Vernon, just wait till you see what your *kinner* have done," Sadie said. "They made these *wunderbar* paintings and we talked about how they feel and…" Sadie realized she was talking too loudly and quickly. She shook her head but couldn't stop smiling. "Thank you for letting the *kinner* do this. I think it's been really *gut* for them."

"I can see that," Vernon said softly. Something in his eyes made Sadie blush.

"Look what I painted, *Daed*!" Lydia leaped from her

seat and ran to her father, her wet canvas paper clutched in her hand.

"Look at mine, *Daed*!" Ned shouted.

"And mine!" Newt said.

Vernon took the time to compliment each child's painting. He started to ask them questions about their paintings but, after sitting still for so long, the children were too restless for any more conversation. "Can we go outside and play?" Newt asked.

"Sure," Vernon said.

"Can I go to the *dawdi haus* and show *Aenti* Arleta my painting?" Lydia asked.

"Ya," Vernon said. "It will be *gut* for you to keep her company for a while."

"I'll *kumme* get you when it's time to help me cook lunch," Sadie said. "We don't want to tire Arleta out. But your *daed*'s right. A short visit would be *gut*."

"Walk your *schwester* over to the *dawdi haus*," Vernon said to the twins. "Then you *buwe* go play."

Sadie felt awkward in the silence after the children raced from the room, whooping and shouting. She wondered what Vernon was thinking. "How much did you hear?" she asked.

"Enough to know that you were right. Art is *gut* for the *kinner*."

Sadie looked down. *"Danki."*

"Nee, I should be thanking you, not the other way around." Vernon stepped closer. Sadie looked back up at him. He returned her gaze and held it. She could feel the intensity of the emotion behind his dark eyes. She swallowed hard. Strange feelings were bubbling up from within her.

"Before you came…" Vernon hesitated. "I'm not *gut* at putting things into words. I'm *gut* at planting and harvesting and fixing broken farm equipment. But when it comes to feelings…"

"It's okay. You don't have to be *gut* at everything. But the truth is, I think you're better at expressing yourself than you think. You said exactly the right things to the *kinner* about their paintings just now. They left here happy because of it."

"They left happy because of what *you* said to them and what you did for them." Vernon's hands moved restlessly as he spoke. "This art therapy stuff… *Ne*, it's more than that. It's you, Sadie. It's everything about you." He stepped closer to Sadie. The masculine scent of leather and wood smoke filled the air around her. Vernon was so close that Sadie could see the lines at the corner of his eyes and the faint sprinkle of freckles across his tan nose. Her heart beat faster.

"You've been a blessing that I haven't deserved, Sadie. I don't know how we survived without you. You've brought joy and life back to this house."

Their eyes were still locked. Sadie could feel her chest rising and falling. She felt so seen, so loved. Vernon leaned closer and Sadie closed her eyes. Time stopped. He was going to kiss her. It was the most wonderful moment of her life.

Then Arleta's voice shouted from across the barn, "Vernon! Are you in here?"

Sadie's eyes flew open and she jerked back from Vernon. Vernon looked at her for a moment, then shook his head. "I'm sorry," he whispered.

Sadie wondered what he meant by that. Was he sorry that he had almost kissed her? Or sorry that Arleta had burst into the barn and he *couldn't* kiss her? Arleta appeared at the tack room door before Sadie could figure it out.

"I've just seen this." Arleta waved a sheet of canvas paper at Vernon.

"*Ach*, Arleta. It's just a painting."

"Lydia was so excited to show you," Sadie added.

"You shouldn't have encouraged her. She's full of pride over it."

"She's just excited," Vernon said. "She's just being a *kind*."

"*Ya*, she's just a child—and a child has to be taught not to have pride. She shouldn't be encouraged to show off."

"That's not what's happening." Vernon removed his straw hat and ran his fingers through his hair. "Can't you see that Sadie is helping the *kinner*?"

"This kind of help is for the *Englisch*. Not for the Amish."

Vernon sighed. Sadie could see he was at a loss for words.

"Ned and Newt talked about their feelings today," Sadie said. "They opened up about the accident and losing their *mamm*. They even talked about you and—"

"You have no business talking about me to the *kinner*."

Sadie shook her head hard. "It wasn't like that. They just need to talk about what happened and how it makes them feel. It could help you too, Arleta. I know how much you must be hurting—"

"You don't know anything about me," Arleta said. "And I will never talk about the accident. Never." Arleta spun around on her heels and stalked away.

Vernon and Sadie stood in silence as they listened to Arleta's footsteps echoing across the barn floor.

"I'm sorry, Sadie," Vernon said.

Sadie put a hand on his arm. "*Nee*, I'm sorry. I only have a few weeks to make a difference here, before *Daed* makes me go home. I really tried to reach Arleta before it was too late, but I don't think it's going to happen. I failed."

"Sadie, after all you've done for the *kinner* and me, you can't possibly believe that you've failed."

"Well, I haven't done enough."

Vernon looked at Sadie with serious eyes. "Sadie, I know you want to help everyone. But sometimes you can't. Sometimes you have to let go and give the person you want to help over to *Gott*. You can't do His job for him."

Sadie frowned. "I didn't mean to…"

"I know. All you've done is to try to help. But you can't force someone to respond the way you want them to. You've got to respect their choice to be the way they are, even though it hurts and makes you so frustrated that some days you feel like you can't—" Vernon let out a sharp breath of air. "Sorry."

"Sounds like you can relate."

"*Ya*. I know how hard it is to watch Arleta refuse to get help. Especially when it's my fault this happened in the first place."

"It wasn't your fault."

"It takes time to believe that."

"Take the time you need. I'll be here, believing in you." Sadie flinched inside. She couldn't believe she had just said that. It was a promise her heart wanted to make, but not something that she should have actually said out loud.

Vernon looked away. "Only until the end of the month…" His eyes darted back to hers. "I don't know what we're going to do after you leave, Sadie. I don't know what *I'm* going to do."

Sadie didn't know how to answer that. She didn't want to think about what would happen when the time came to leave. She didn't think she could bear to go.

Chapter Twelve

The Kauffman buggy pulled up to Mary King's small white clapboard house. Today was a church Sunday and it was Mary's turn to host this week. Vernon was surprised that he didn't feel that familiar tightness in his chest as he looked at the gathering crowd. A row of men in black hats and black coats stood near Mary's barn, talking in low voices and chuckling. Groups of women chatted together, their blue, green and purple cape dresses creating a splash of color against the plain white house. Children dressed in their Sunday best played quietly in the shade of a maple tree.

Vernon parked alongside the gray buggies that lined Mary's front yard. Mary's nephew Gabriel King had lived with her until recently, when he moved out to marry Eliza Zook. Vernon wondered how Mary was handling living alone. He figured she must be in her early thirties. He had heard that lots of *Englisch* women married in their thirties, but in the Amish community, Mary had passed the age when a woman could expect a proposal. Vernon sensed the loneliness behind the perfect facade of her neatly kept yard, sparkling clean, whitewashed house and welcoming smile. Vernon had given up on keeping that facade in his own life long ago. He wondered how Mary managed. Before Sadie came in his life, he couldn't bear to—

Vernon cut off the thought. He had allowed his boundaries to blur and now his relationship with Sadie had become dangerously close to something beyond friendship. He was feeling emotions toward her that he had not felt since he lost Lorna. Vernon waited for the steel door to close around his heart in response to that swell of emotion. But instead, he felt a curious peace, even as he saw the crowd surrounding him. What was happening to him?

Sadie Lapp, that's what.

Voices called out to Vernon from across the yard as people began to notice his arrival. Bishop Amos and Levi Miller hurried over to welcome the family. Viola and Edna rushed over to greet Arleta, who managed a small smile. Ned and Newt endured pats on the head and a pinch on the cheek from Viola before they managed to escape. They made a beeline for Simon Miller, whose black best-for-Sunday pants already had mud stains on the knees. Vernon did not have time to worry about what trouble his sons might get into before the service started. He was too busy fending off Viola, who was never afraid to ask questions that nobody else would.

"Vernon, how are you?" she asked as she squinted at him through her bifocals.

"Fine, thanks," he answered.

"No, really. How *are* you?"

"Like I said, fine."

Viola made a sound in the back of her throat. "Now, Vernon, don't you dismiss me." She stepped closer and craned her neck to meet his eyes. "I see a change in you, ain't so? You're looking much better. That old frown of yours isn't so severe today. Sadie's having a *gut* influence, *ya*?"

Vernon shot a self-conscious glance at Sadie, who stood beside him, holding Lydia's hand. "I, uh, well, she's been a wonderful good *kinnsmaad*."

Viola raised an eyebrow. "I think that she's been a *gut* influence on more than just the *kinner*."

Vernon shifted his weight from one foot to the other. He wasn't used to someone being so forward about relationships. But Viola had a way of knowing how people felt about one another even before *they* did. It was her most helpful—and most annoying—talent. "*Ach*, well, I better check on my *buwe*." He looked past Viola to where Simon and his twins huddled around a mud puddle. "I don't know what they're doing, but they're probably up to no *gut*."

"And, with Simon here, whatever they're doing probably involves an amphibian or two," Sadie added.

Vernon chuckled. Everyone knew about Simon's love for creepy-crawly creatures. "For sure and certain."

"Humph." Viola tapped her cane on the hard earth. "You can change the subject, Vernon Kauffman, but you can't change the facts."

"I don't know what you mean," Vernon said. He hoped that didn't count as a lie. He did feel confused about his feelings, so there was truth in the statement.

Viola's eyes narrowed. She grabbed his elbow and pulled him closer to her, until he bent down to her height. "Don't push Sadie away like you do everyone else, Vernon," she whispered in his ear. "This might be your last chance."

Viola's warning sent a shockwave through him and he straightened back up quickly. Viola gave a satisfied nod before she hobbled away with a smug smile.

Vernon made sure that Arleta was settled on the women's side of the room before he found a seat with the men. It felt right to be among the faithful, singing the old hymns and remembering there was something bigger out there than his own life. How had he gotten so far from that realization?

He felt like he had been underwater for months and was just coming up to the surface to breathe again.

Vernon glanced up from his copy of the *Ausbund*—the old Amish hymnal—and looked across the room at Sadie. She stood close to Arleta, moving her finger under the words as they sang to help Arleta keep her place. Lydia clung to the skirt of Sadie's dress, humming along with the words she couldn't read. Vernon's heart swelled at Sadie's thoughtfulness. And not just for her kindness toward Arleta and his children, but for her ability to make him feel a part of the community again. Somehow, she had reminded him that he wasn't such an outsider, after all. Maybe it was because she didn't quite fit in, but she still believed she deserved a place among the Amish of Bluebird Hills. If she could believe that, despite her differences, then maybe he could too.

The chorus of rich, a cappella voices filled Mary King's living room. The space was tight, but like other Amish homes, the house had been built with a longer than standard living room in order to accommodate church services. The men had moved Mary's old upholstered chair, wooden rocking chairs and clunky propane lamp into her bedroom to clear up space. The portable benches took up all of the empty room, but the close quarters only added to the coziness of the service.

After Bishop Amos's two sermons, and several more songs, the three-hour service wound to a close. Ned and Newt could not jump up fast enough. Vernon had managed to keep them from squirming too much, but it was a relief to let them run free. The men would line up to eat first, so his sons had some time to blow off steam in Mary's yard with the other boys before it was their turn.

Vernon caught sight of Sadie while he moved through

the buffet line, heaping his plate full of sliced meat, cheese, pickled vegetables, bread with peanut butter church spread and a big slice of shoofly pie. She stayed close to Arleta as they poured mugs of black coffee for the men. It was clear that Sadie was watching out for his sister and helping her navigate the bustling atmosphere.

When Vernon reached the end of the line, he noticed Sadie and Arleta whispering, then Sadie nodded and placed a reassuring hand on Arleta's arm. Arleta frowned and scurried out of the kitchen, into the hot July sun. Vernon managed to catch Sadie's eye across the crowded kitchen and she crossed the room to him, a mug of coffee in her hand. "Here," she said as she handed him the mug. "*Gut* service, *ya*?"

"*Ya*," Vernon said, holding her gaze. He felt himself falling into her clear blue eyes. He wanted to tell her that everything felt different since she had come into his life and that, for the first time since Lorna passed away, he felt at home during a service again. Instead, he cleared his throat and looked away. "How's Arleta doing? She usually gets overstimulated in situations like this. It's pretty crowded and noisy in here."

Sadie nodded. "She's going to take a break and get some fresh air. Someone needs to check on the *buwe*, anyway."

Vernon nodded. "*Ya*, that's *gut* for her to get away for a few minutes. I hope she's not still upset…" He glanced from side to side, then leaned closer to Sadie and lowered his voice. "About the painting."

Sadie frowned. "Honestly, I can feel the tension there. It's not so *gut* between us." Sadie gave a little laugh, but her eyes did not smile. "But when is it ever? It did feel like she was starting to warm up to me, but now…" Sadie shrugged. "I feel like we've taken a step backward. I don't know what to do."

"Just keep being yourself. You'll reach her. How could you not? You have a gift for reaching people."

Sadie froze. "You really think so?"

Vernon hesitated, then said what he was feeling. "You reached me, didn't you?" His stomach leaped into his throat as soon as the words left his mouth. He couldn't believe he had just said that out loud. But sharing the truth with Sadie felt so right that he couldn't resist. And the way her face lit up at his admission was all the reward he needed. It didn't matter how uncomfortable and exposed he felt, he had made Sadie feel good about herself and that was what mattered.

Sadie could not believe what she had just heard. Did Vernon just admit that she had reached him? She had felt them growing closer over the past few days—and he had nearly kissed her—but she had only dared to hope that he felt as transformed as she did by their burgeoning relationship.

Now she knew he felt the same way.

Sadie could not stop the grin that overtook her face. She felt a rush of joy all the way from her head to the tips of her toes. There was so much she wanted to say, but she just stood there, staring at Vernon and beaming.

He smiled back and gave her a wink that made her knees weak. Then he disappeared into the crowd to find a seat in the living room with the men to eat his meal. Sadie was left reeling, her mind full of exciting questions. With Vernon opening up about his feelings for her, Arleta was the only barrier left between them. Surely Sadie could reach her too, just like Vernon said. How hard could it be, now that she had Vernon's full support?

A warning in the pit of her stomach whispered that it

might not be so easy. Sadie had tried to convince herself all morning that things were okay between her and Arleta, but after their heated discussion in the barn, Arleta had become more distant than ever. Sadie had tried to be more accommodating to make up for the falling-out, but this seemed to only offend Arleta more. But what else could Sadie do? It was clear that Arleta was struggling being in the crowded house and Sadie couldn't just abandon her. How could something so straightforward become so complicated? Shouldn't it be easy to offer someone support?

Sadie thought about her dilemma as she poured more cups of hot black coffee for the men.

"Careful," an elderly voice piped up from behind Sadie.

Sadie jolted back to the present and realized she was about to overfill a mug of coffee. "*Danki*, Viola," she said, then laughed as she set down the carafe. "I don't know where my head is today." Sadie glanced over her shoulder to where Viola stood behind her with both hands resting on her cane, hunched forward in her usual posture.

"It's on either Vernon or Arleta, *ya*?" Viola said in a matter-of-fact tone, as if it were completely obvious.

"You're right. I was thinking about Arleta." Sadie smiled and shook her head as she reached for another empty mug to fill. "How did you know?"

"Because I wasn't born yesterday, dear." Viola pointed her cane in the direction of the kitchen window. "And Arleta is having a pretty serious conversation with the bishop out there. She looks pretty upset over something and so do you."

Sadie glanced out the window. Arleta and Bishop Amos stood beneath a maple tree in the backyard. Arleta was frowning and gesturing. Amos looked concerned. As Sadie watched, he took off his straw hat, wiped the sweat from his head, then replaced his hat. She could hear the sound of their voices drifting through the open window but couldn't make out the words. Sadie sighed and turned her attention back to the coffee. Her stomach tightened at the thought of what Arleta might be telling Amos, and Sadie didn't want to think about it.

"Arleta and I just can't find common ground. I've really tried and I don't know what else to do."

"You don't see things quite the same way as most folks around here, ain't so?" Viola's expression showed she already knew the answer.

"That's true."

"And that's *oll recht*, as long as you don't take it too far. We all have to follow the rules." Viola held up her pointer finger and shook it in the air. "It's interpreting those rules that can be tricky sometimes."

Sadie nodded, unsure of how to respond.

"The *Ordnung* spells out a lot of things—the length of our dress, the measurements of our *kapp*, the way we wear our hair. But are your paintings worldly? The *Ordnung* doesn't say exactly… And different folks feel differently about it."

"How did you know that Arleta—"

"I already told you, I wasn't born yesterday. I know Arleta and I know she isn't the creative type. Remember that not everyone thinks like you, Sadie. Some people are comforted by rules and tradition just like you're comforted by art. There's nothing wrong with that."

"Of course not. I'm Amish. I follow the rules and keep the traditions. I know they're *gut*."

"But you don't feel them *here* the way Arleta does." Viola tapped her own chest, over her heart. "I'm guessing that you feel closer to *Gott* when you're painting then when you're thinking about the rules."

Sadie's mouth dropped open. Viola knew exactly how she felt.

Viola gave her a dismissive wave of a hand. "Don't stand there gaping like a trout."

Sadie snapped her mouth shut.

"Here's what you have to remember. Rules make Arleta feel safe. They bring order to her life. She needs to know what to expect each day. Not everyone likes to flit around, experiencing new things all the time, you know."

"Oh. I didn't mean—"

"I know you didn't mean to judge Arleta or think your way of seeing things is better. Just remember that Arleta has just as much right to feel the way she does about art as you do. If you really believe that everyone should think for themselves, then let her think for herself."

Sadie felt stung. Had she been trying to force Arleta into a box that she didn't belong in? Was she trying to make Arleta see the world through Sadie's eyes, instead of the way Arleta wanted to see the world?

"Just because Arleta is disabled doesn't mean she can't think for herself. You have to respect that. She hasn't lost the right to have her own complicated and unique personality."

Sadie let out a long, frustrated exhale. "I thought I was helping."

"And I'm sure you have been." Viola reached out and gave Sadie's hand a reassuring pat. "But even the best intentions can go off track. That's why I'm here."

Sadie managed a slight smile. Despite all her quirks, Viola almost always hit the mark. "What would we do without you, Viola?"

Viola looked up to the heavens with a long-suffering expression. "I can only imagine."

Ada appeared at Viola's shoulder to ask if anyone had seen the salt shaker. Viola hobbled away, leaving Sadie to catch up with her mother and sisters as they finished their jobs in the kitchen. But even though the conversation was lighthearted, Sadie's heart felt heavy after her conversation with Viola.

When all the men, women and children had taken their turn eating, Sadie returned to the kitchen with the other women to clean up from the meal. She dried dishes while Mary King washed them in the big sink beneath the open window. A hot July breeze carrying the scent of fresh-cut grass billowed into the room while they worked.

Sadie wondered how Mary was doing now that she lived alone, but she wasn't sure it was okay to ask. She didn't want to seem like she was prying, but she worried that Mary's eyes looked sad. Sadie, for all her natural cheerfulness, knew how sharp loneliness could feel, especially when surrounded by other people.

Lydia clung to Sadie's side for a while, then decided that it would be more fun to join the other children outside. The men clustered beneath the shade of the maple trees, chatting about the health of the summer crops and an upcoming livestock auction in a neighboring church district. Occasionally, the shouts of young boys would punctuate the peaceful Sunday atmosphere and one of the fathers would shoot his son a stern look from across the yard. Usually that father was Vernon and the rambunctious boys were Ned and Newt.

Sadie suppressed a smile as she watched Ned and Newt playing with Simon through the kitchen window. The three boys looked deep in concentration as they dug in the dirt, apparently looking for something. Sadie decided she didn't want to know what they hoped to find. Earthworms probably. She just hoped that any worms they found didn't end up in her bed that night.

Then it hit her that it had been a long time since the twins had tried to drive her away. Instead, they seemed to want her to stay now. It was only Arleta who had a problem with Sadie...

"Excuse me, Sadie. Can I talk to you, please?"

Sadie startled at the sound of the bishop's voice.

"Of course." Sadie tried to sound cheerful, but an alarm went off inside. Could this have to do with the conversation Arleta had had with the bishop earlier? "Mary, can you manage?" Sadie finished wiping the plate in her hand and set it on top of a stack of dried dishes.

"I'll take over," Ada said, sliding in to take Sadie's place beside the sink. *"Danki, Mamm."* Sadie thought she caught a flicker of concern in her mother's eye as she passed her the dish towel but hoped it was just her imagination.

Sadie followed Bishop Amos outside. Vernon straightened up when he saw them walking together. He watched them cross the yard with a frown on his face.

"We'll meet in the barn," Amos said as he led the way. Sadie felt like everyone was staring as she followed him. Surely it was her imagination. Or were people whispering about her as she passed by? She felt her face heat up from more than the afternoon sun.

When they walked into the barn, Sadie was surprised to see a row of chairs set out, as if there was a gathering planned. Arleta and the church elders were all seated in silence, apparently waiting for her. The sinking feeling in Sadie's stomach deepened.

"Why don't you have a seat?" Amos asked as he gestured to the empty chair.

The earthy scent of hay surrounded Sadie as she sat down. Mary's buggy horse snorted and stamped a hoof from inside its stall. Sadie looked over to see the horse watching her. Were even the farm animals staring at her now?

"We need to talk," Amos said as he took the chair opposite Sadie. But before he could say more, the barn door creaked open and Vernon strode in. Disturbed by the sudden movement, a bird in the rafters took flight and disappeared through the hayloft window with a loud fluttering of wings. Vernon furrowed his brows when he saw Arleta and the elders. His eyes flicked from Amos to Sadie, then back to Amos. "Everything *oll recht*?" he asked.

"Nee," Arleta said.

"Perhaps," Amos said at the same time.

They glanced at one another and Arleta frowned. Amos raised his hands. "Let's hear what everyone has to say."

"Say about what?" Vernon asked. He crossed his arms.

"About Sadie breaking the *Ordnung*," Arleta said.

Sadie's body tightened. It was as she had feared. Would she be shunned for this? For how long? Where would she go? Even if it was only a month's shunning, she didn't think she could bear to be isolated for that long.

"Now, wait a minute—" Vernon's expression hardened as he moved protectively toward Sadie.

Amos put up his hand. "Let's discuss this in an orderly fashion. You can stay if you like, as long as it's *oll recht* with Sadie."

"I'd like Vernon to stay," Sadie said.

Vernon gave a tight nod. There weren't any empty chairs left, so he walked to where Sadie sat and stood behind her. She could feel the quiet strength of his presence and it gave her courage to face the situation. She twisted her head to peer up at him and mouthed *Danki*.

He placed a warm, firm hand on her shoulder in response. How had Vernon Kauffman become such a source of comfort? Was this the man who had made her too nervous to speak when she had first arrived at his farm?

"Arleta, why don't you tell us what's bothering you?" Amos asked.

Sadie turned her attention back to Amos and the elders. *Please have your will in this, Gott*, she said in silent prayer as she clasped her hands together to keep them from shaking and revealing her fear.

"It's not that something's bothering me," Arleta said. "It's that Sadie is breaking the rules. The truth is, I like Sadie."

Sadie stiffened at this revelation. This was certainly news to her.

"She's a nice girl and she means well, I'm sure," Arleta continued. "But she's leading our family astray, despite her *gut* intentions."

"Arleta, can you even hear what you're saying? I can't believe—"

"You'll have to wait your turn, Vernon," Amos interrupted.

Vernon clenched his jaw in an effort to hold his tongue.

"She's been teaching the *kinner* to paint," Arleta said.

One of the elders grunted and another shook his head.

"She says it's helping them, but it's tempting them to *hoochmut*. You should have seen how proud Lydia was to show me the painting she made. I don't have to tell you how serious the sin of pride is. We know that, as Amish, we are called to live Plain lives."

A wave of murmurs and nods passed through the room.

"And what about graven images?" Arleta went on. "Sadie says she doesn't do that, but where do you draw the line? Now it's landscapes, but couldn't that lead to images of people? It's best to stay away from anything that's questionable—anything that could potentially lead to sin. It's a slippery slope, *ya*?"

Amos stroked his long gray beard in thoughtful silence. His expression gave nothing away.

"And here's another thing," Arleta said. She leaned forward in her seat as her emotions rose. "It's worldly. Painting just isn't something that *gut* Amish folk do. It's something that fancy *Englischers* do. It just isn't right. Sadie needs to separate herself from the world. And she certainly needs to keep my niece and nephews away from that sort of worldliness." Arleta leaned back in her chair. She thought for a moment, then exhaled. "I guess that's about it."

Well, Sadie thought, *that's more than enough to get me shunned, at least for a time.*

Amos nodded at Arleta, the turned his gaze on Sadie. Sadie could sense that ever-present kindness behind his eyes, but there was a distance there too. He seemed to be bracing himself to make a difficult decision. "Sadie, what would you like to say in response to that?"

Sadie tried to order her thoughts, but her heart beat too fast and her brain swirled with arguments that she didn't know how to put into words. Vernon's hand gently squeezed her shoulder. "I understand where Arleta is coming from," Sadie said after the awkward moment of silence. "She has a right to feel that way about painting. It's *gut* to err on the side of caution when it comes to sin."

The elders nodded.

"But so many things can tempt us to sin, that we can't avoid them all. A *gut* crop of wheat, a cow that produces more milk than the neighbor's cow, a family blessed with lots of children—these are all *gut* things from *Gott*, but they could all lead to *hoochmut,* if we approach them the wrong way in our heart."

One of the elders nodded. Amos ran his fingers through his beard as he listened intently.

"That's beside the point," Arleta said. "You can't avoid those things, but you can avoid painting."

Sadie looked down. "You're right." She studied her hands, clasped tightly in her lap. "But I keep all the rules spelled out in the *Ordnung.* I'm very careful. I've never been in trouble for that."

"That's true," Amos said.

"The *Ordnung* doesn't say anything about painting," Sadie said.

"It doesn't have to," Arleta cut in. "It goes without saying—it's obvious."

"But when everything else is spelled out, wouldn't this be too, if it were too worldly?"

Amos sighed. "We've never had to deal with this issue before. That's why it's not spelled out in the rules for our church district. You're the first church member in our district who has wanted to paint. It's...unusual."

"Which makes it wrong," Arleta said. "We should all strive to keep traditions. If no one in our district has done it before, it must be too worldly." Arleta threw up her hands. "It's just common sense! We don't change the way we've always done things. And there's a reason for that! What's next? Driving cars and using electricity in our homes?"

Amos made a small motion with his hand to communicate the need for silence.

"I don't know what else to say..." Sadie swallowed hard and gathered her courage. "Except that I feel closest to *Gott* when I paint. I feel connected to the beauty of His creation when I capture it on canvas."

Arleta made a sharp noise of disapproval in the back of her throat.

"I'd like to say something," Vernon said.

The sound of his deep, even voice sent a shiver of hope down Sadie's spine.

Amos nodded his agreement.

Vernon stepped around from behind Sadie's chair to face the elders. "I don't pretend to have all the answers. I can't understand *Gott* or his ways. All I know is that my family has been healing since Sadie came. That's a *gut* thing. A blessing."

Arleta shifted uncomfortably in her seat. One of the elders frowned in concentration.

"You all know the tragedy that my family's been through. We were in a dark place when Sadie came to us. And now, it feels like the clouds have broken and we can see the sun again. She got my *buwe* to behave and Lydia isn't so clingy anymore. Lydia feels safe enough to spend time alone again. And, Sadie helped me…" Vernon looked down and cleared his throat. "*Ach*, well, she's shown me how to live again. After we lost Lorna, I had forgotten how."

Sadie couldn't believe that Vernon had said those words out loud to the church leaders. Everything in her wanted to leap up and sing. No matter what Amos and the elders decided today, she knew everything would be okay because she and Vernon were connected. And that connection could not be broken.

"It's true that Sadie painted with my *kinner*. She tried— we both tried—to get Arleta to join them. There's a thing called art therapy, you see. And after everything they've been through because of the accident, we thought that getting their feelings out through artwork might help them.

All of them. It's *gut* for emotional healing and healing from head injuries."

"Sadie isn't an art therapist," Arleta said. "That's an *Englisch* job."

"That's true," Vernon said. "She doesn't have a degree in it, of course. But she never claimed to be an actual art therapist. She just knows that painting your feelings helps and she wanted to give that gift to our family. So she did what she could to show them how to use painting for healing. It wasn't a worldly thing. It wasn't about pride. It was about helping our family."

Amos ran his fingers through his beard. After a few beats of silence, he nodded. "And did it help?"

"For sure and certain," Vernon said. "I can't explain it, but getting their emotions out on canvas paper seemed to really help. The *buwe* even opened up about how they felt about the accident. They've never been willing to talk about that before. I know they still have a long way to go, but painting with Sadie—and just being cared for by her—has been a really *gut* start. I feel like things are going to be *oll recht* now."

Vernon looked surprised to have spoken as much as he had. He blinked and his expression became guarded. "That's all I have to say."

Sadie knew he had put himself out there for her sake, to defend her. Her heart swelled with love for him. He had made himself vulnerable, in front of all the church leaders, just for her.

"You've given us a lot to think about," Amos said.

The elders murmured and nodded.

"Give us some time to discuss this. We'll let you know when we've made a decision about the matter."

Sadie wanted to ask Amos questions. Were they considering shunning her? Would they ban her from painting? What about the fact that Amos had allowed her to sell her paintings in Aunt Fannie's Amish Gifts up to now? Would they take that away from her, since she had encouraged others to paint?

How could this be happening, when all she had wanted to do was help people who were hurting?

Chapter Thirteen

Sadie stood beneath the shade of one of Mary King's maple trees, twisting her hands as she waited to hear the elders' decision. Vernon stood beside her, his quiet presence comforting her. Sunlight filtered through the maple leaves and dappled the grass with soft yellow splotches. June bugs buzzed around them in the humid air and the laughter of children drifted across the yard. It would be a pleasant summer afternoon, if it weren't for the dread that filled Sadie's heart.

"What's this I am hearing?" Sadie turned to see her father, Abram, barreling toward her. Ada followed close behind, her baby bouncing on her hip as she tried to keep up on legs that were much shorter and plumper than her husband's. She kept one hand on her *kapp* to keep it in place as she hurried.

"It's *oll recht, Daed.*" Sadie tried to sound confident, but her stomach sank in protest, even as she said the words.

Abram's eyes narrowed. "Not if you've been breaking the *Ordnung.*"

Ada reached them and put a hand on Abram's arm. "Give her a chance to explain," she said as she caught her breath.

"What's there to explain?" Abram stared down at his daughter with hard eyes. "Are you breaking the *Ordnung*? It's a simple yes or no answer."

Sadie shrunk back. Her mind reeled with explanations, but all her words stuck in her throat at the sight of her father's disapproval.

Vernon stepped forward. "She's not breaking the rules," he said evenly. "And everything she's done has been to help my family and me. I can vouch for her."

Abram stared at Vernon for a few beats. His eyes narrowed.

"She's been a blessing, Abram." Vernon held Abram's hard gaze without flinching. Then he took another step closer to Sadie. She turned and looked up at him. Their eyes met and he gave a reassuring nod that flooded her chest with warmth. The thought of her father's disapproval still sent a sharp wave of panic through her but, with Vernon by her side, Sadie felt strong enough to face it.

Vernon maintained that warm, steady eye contact for a long moment. When Sadie broke it to look back at her father, she could sense a shift in Abram's attitude. His expression looked harder, his eyes narrower, as he sized them both up. "I don't like what I'm seeing," he said.

"At least wait until we hear back from the elders before you get upset." Sadie's face took on a pleading look. "They might say everything is *oll recht*."

"I don't think everything is *oll recht*—even if the elders give you permission to keep painting."

"I don't understand," Sadie said. "If the elders say—"

"We will discuss this later," Abram interrupted. "I can see there is more to be concerned about here than just your artwork." He shook his head, shot Vernon a blistering look of disapproval and turned on his heels. "Let's go, Ada," he said as he marched away. "The evening chores won't wait."

Ada enveloped Sadie in a quick hug. The baby squirmed

and gurgled between them. "*Gott* will work this all for *gut*. Just wait and see."

"But, *Daed*…"

Ada pulled back from the hug but kept her hand on Sadie's arm as she looked her daughter in the eye. "Your father sees everything in black-and-white. He can't always understand your perspective. But he only wants the best for you. He's afraid you'll lose your way. He just wants to make sure you stay true to our Amish faith."

"I do, *Mamm*."

"I know. But it's hard for him to see that when you approach things so differently than he does. He's afraid for you, Sadie. That's why he seems angry." Ada leaned forward and pecked her daughter on the cheek. "He loves you, even though he'll never be able to say it out loud. This is how he shows it."

Sadie watched as her mother hurried after Abram. She called to her children as she crossed the yard and a handful of girls and boys stopped playing to fall into line behind her. Sadie kept watching as her family gathered beside their buggy and her father took the horse's lead in hand. She sighed and turned away. "There are better ways to show love than this," she murmured.

"Ya," Vernon said. "But I've acted the same way. It isn't easy to show your *kinner* how you really feel."

"That doesn't make it *oll recht*."

"Nee." Vernon looked thoughtful. "It's not an excuse. Just an explanation. Maybe your *daed* will learn how to communicate his feelings in a better way, one day." He swallowed and looked at her. "You helped me to do that."

Sadie opened her mouth to respond. There was so much she wanted to say to Vernon. But Amos's voice interrupted her. "There you two are." He strode toward them. "We've made a decision."

All thoughts flew from Sadie's head.

Amos smiled and the corners of his eyes crinkled. "You haven't gone against our ways."

Sadie exhaled as the tension released from her body in a hot rush.

Amos nodded toward Vernon. "He gave a *gut* argument on your behalf."

"What about Arleta?" Vernon asked.

"I'll speak to her next," Amos said. "She meant well." Amos spread his hands out, palms up. "Arleta just wanted to keep the *kinner* on a *gut* path. She did the right thing to *kumme* to us. Better safe than sorry, *ya*?"

Vernon rubbed a hand over his forehead. He looked relieved, but tired. "*Danki*, Amos. We best be getting on home now."

Amos gave Vernon a firm pat on the back. "I hope to see you again soon, Vernon. It's *gut* that you're getting out again."

"We'll visit this Sunday."

Amos gave a genuine smile that brightened his entire face. "Nothing would make me happier, Vernon. *Gott* is doing *gut* things for you and your family."

"With a few complications thrown in," Vernon said as his eyes flicked across the yard to where Arleta stood alone with her arms crossed.

Amos chuckled. "Trust *Gott*, Vernon. His path isn't always easy, but it's always *gut*."

Vernon's stomach twisted and turned. He wanted to scoop Sadie into his arms and defend her against anyone who came against her.

But Arleta was his sister. And he owed her everything

after his terrible mistake cost her nearly everything. What could he possibly do about this situation?

Old Max's hooves beat a steady rhythm down the country highway as they headed home. Ears of feed corn waved in the breeze alongside the road and the occasional car zipped past them, blowing up a hot wind that sent Sadie's *kapp* strings flying. The children bounced and shouted in the back of the buggy, while Arleta stayed silent throughout the ride. Vernon could sense Sadie's stress at having to share a buggy with her.

Vernon kept thinking he needed to say something—*anything*—but nothing reasonable came to mind. So he watched Old Max plodding along and kept his mouth shut. By the time they reached the farm, Vernon couldn't leap from the buggy fast enough. All he wanted was to disappear into the barn and escape from the situation. He needed to comfort Sadie, but how could he balance that with his need to accommodate Arleta?

His heart tugged within him, telling him to turn toward Sadie, that she was his future and that Arleta would understand, somehow. But his mind fought within him as the guilt rose. Vernon couldn't look either woman in the eye as he helped them from the buggy, then rushed to get Old Max unhitched. Maybe if he avoided the situation long enough, it would just go away.

It didn't. Instead, Sadie cornered him in the barn less than an hour later.

"I thought I'd find you here," she said in a quiet voice. Her usual smile was missing.

Vernon grunted and kept pitching fresh hay into Big Red's stall. The draft horse was spending the afternoon under the sun in the south pasture, where he could stretch his legs and enjoy fresh green grass on his day off.

"You've been out here a long time for a Sunday," Sadie said. "You're not doing more chores than you have to, are you?"

"Big Red has to have a clean stall, Sabbath or not."

"Hmm." Sadie didn't look convinced. "So you're not taking extra time in order to avoid us?" One eyebrow raised to punctuate the question.

"Humph."

Sadie laughed. The sound made Vernon relax a little. "The best you can do is 'humph'?" she asked.

"Yep." He couldn't help shooting Sadie a smile. "Best I can do."

Sadie looked amused before her face dropped back to a serious expression. "Can we talk?"

Vernon puffed out his cheeks and exhaled. "Uh, sure." He lifted the pitchfork, swung it around and dropped a load of hay onto the floor of the stall.

Sadie stepped closer. "I mean, can you stop working for a minute and pay attention to the conversation, please?"

Vernon lowered the pitchfork and leaned it against the wall, then squeezed his eyes shut and pinched the bridge of his nose. He could feel a headache coming on. Before Sadie came, no one challenged him to talk about conflicts or emotions. He had seen the difference it made, but right now he just wanted to get away from it all. "Sure," he said, eyes still closed.

Sadie waited until he dropped his hand and opened his eyes. *"Gut."* She took a deep breath and raised her chin. Vernon could tell she was nervous to confront him, but she hid it well. "It's obvious you're avoiding us. That's not going to help anything."

Vernon shifted his weight from one foot to the other.

"Sure it will. I don't have to deal with the problem if I'm not around it."

"Vernon, you know what I mean."

Vernon looked down. "*Ya*. I know." He scratched his beard. "But I can't talk to Arleta right now. She went after you and that…" He glanced at Sadie, then away again. "That's not *oll recht*." There was so much more he wanted to say. He wanted to explain that his feelings for Sadie were so strong that he had to defend her—even against his own sister. But he couldn't. So he skipped over that. "I can't talk to her because I have to be loyal to her—I owe that to her. But after this…" He shook his head. "I'm pretty upset, but I can't say what I want to. Does that make sense?"

"Of course it does. But avoiding her isn't going to solve the problem or make anyone feel any better."

"We've been doing fine so far."

Sadie shot him a look. "Have you?"

"Okay. Not really."

"The longer you put it off, the worse it's going to feel when you finally talk to her."

"I could just put it off forever."

"Vernon."

Vernon lifted his hands in surrender. "*Oll recht. Oll recht.* I'll talk to her."

"*Gut.* You won't be sorry."

"We'll see about that," Vernon muttered, but then he shot her a half smile to show he was joking. He picked the pitchfork back up and went for another load of hay. Sadie didn't move. Vernon sighed and leaned the pitchfork against the wall again. "You mean right now, don't you. And you're not going to leave until I do, are you?"

"Right on both counts."

"Well, I guess that settles it. Let's get this over with."

"You know, Vernon, talking out your problems isn't so bad once you actually do it," Sadie said as they began walking across the barn together. "You're making it a lot worse than it has to be."

Vernon gave her a look. "Have *you* ever talked to Arleta about your problems with one another?"

"Um, no. Not really." Sadie flashed a sheepish grin. "Okay. You got me. But still, it won't be so bad."

"We'll see about that."

Vernon found Arleta in the *dawdi haus*, where he expected she would be. The dead vines on the trellis had been cut back, the hedges trimmed and the floorboards of the porch freshly scrubbed—obviously Sadie's work. The little house felt like a cozy cottage again, the air of sadness lifted.

Vernon knocked, then cracked open the door. "Can I *kumme* in?"

Arleta sat in her glider, hands folded, eyes closed. "I'm resting," she said. "It's been a big day."

"Ya." Vernon tried not to sound as harsh as he wanted to. "That's certain sure." The green blinds were drawn as usual, but Vernon could see in the dim light that the small parlor had been mopped, dusted and swept—another sign of Sadie's efforts. "I don't want to bother you, but I think we need to talk."

"Talk? When do we ever talk?"

"Not much." Vernon stepped inside and quietly closed the door behind him. "I think it's time we started."

Arleta snorted. "Just keep it down so I don't get one of my headaches."

"Oll recht," Vernon whispered. He moved Arleta's knitting basket from the sofa and sat down. Neither sibling spoke for a moment. "That's a pretty quilt," Vernon said

as he nodded toward the quilt rack. "Did you just finish that one?"

"Vernon, I know you're not here to talk about quilting. Just get on with it."

"Right." Vernon exhaled. "I don't like what you did today."

"I did the right thing."

"Sadie trusted you. She came here to help us and you tried to get her shunned." Vernon stood up and began pacing the room. Between his long legs and the short length of the room, he could only walk three strides before having to spin around and pace in the opposite direction. "You shouldn't have hurt her like that."

"Hurt her?" Arleta stiffened. "I'm protecting her and your *kinner*. We don't have rules to hurt people. We have rules because they're *gut* for us. Remember what it means to be Amish, Vernon. Don't let her influence you to go astray."

Vernon reached the beadboard wall, spun around and kept pacing. "Amos and the elders say she didn't break the *Ordnung*."

Arleta nodded. "So no harm is done."

Vernon skidded to a stop. "No harm done? You've humiliated her in front of the entire church district. You've made her feel like she doesn't belong."

"*Nee*. I was doing what a *gut* Amish friend should do— keeping someone I love on the right path."

Vernon squinted at Arleta. "Did you say *love*?"

"*Ya.*" Arleta pursed her lips and reached for her knitting basket.

"Are you trying to say that you consider Sadie a friend?"

"I suppose so." She rummaged in the basket and pulled out a ball of gray yarn. "She's been *gut* to us, ain't so? You just said so yourself."

Vernon began pacing again. "But…" He crossed the room

and back. "You didn't want her to *kumme* and you've acted like she's in the way ever since she came."

"It's true I didn't want her to *kumme* here. But we've had *gut* times together since she arrived."

"You sure don't show it," Vernon muttered.

"Ha! You're one to talk, Vernon. You've been avoiding me for months. You barely spoke to the *kinner* or me before Sadie came."

"That's not true."

"*Ya*, it is."

"Okay, but it's not true for the reason that you think."

"Then why don't you explain."

Vernon's hands tightened into fists as he paced. "I can't."

"Vernon, stop being so *rutschy* and sit down. All that pacing is making me dizzy."

"I'm restless because I can't explain how I feel to you." Vernon stalked to the couch and flung himself down. "I've avoided you because I feel too guilty to face you." There, he had said it. He braced his elbows on his knees and covered his face with his hands. "It's my fault, Arleta. It's all my fault."

Silence filled the room. Arleta's glider whined. A bird chirped in the oak tree outside the window. "I didn't have to get in that buggy," Arleta said finally.

"I didn't leave you much choice."

"It was up to me," Arleta said quietly. She stared down at the ball of yarn in her hand.

"I never should have driven that night."

"*Nee*, you shouldn't have. And I've blamed you for it."

Vernon's chest contracted. He couldn't bear to hear those words. It was as he had feared. He wished he had never tried to talk to Arleta.

"But that's because it was easier than blaming myself."

Vernon dropped his hands and his face shot up. His gaze pierced Arleta's. "What?"

"You heard me. I've been so angry at myself for getting in that buggy, for not being able to stop you, for everything. I shifted that anger to you instead, so I could keep going. If I blame you, I don't have to live with the pain of blaming myself."

"But it wasn't your fault."

Arleta took a deep breath and let it out slowly. "Maybe it wasn't anybody's fault. That's why they call it an accident. And even if you do bear some responsibility for it, what *gut* does it do any of us for you to hold on to that guilt?"

"I don't know how to stop blaming myself," Vernon said quietly.

"Listen to Sadie. She's given you a *gut* start on it."

Vernon frowned. "But you believe she's a bad influence. You're not making sense."

"*Ach*, well, she's too creative and free-spirited. But overall…" Arleta shrugged. "She's been *gut* for this family. The *kinner* are happier. You're happier. Maybe I am too, just a little."

"Maybe more than just a little," Vernon said with a teasing smile.

"Don't push it, Vernon."

Vernon chuckled. "*Oll recht*. But I still don't get it. You just reported her to the church leaders, and now you're saying she's *gut* for us?"

Arleta looked at Vernon like he was dim. "It makes perfect sense. Bishop Amos and the elders said she didn't break the rules."

"So that's it? You're okay with her painting now?"

"Of course. They say it's okay, so it's okay."

"But…" Vernon shook his head.

"Listen, I follow the rules. The rules are *gut*. They are there to protect us, to guide us and keep us right with *Gott*. One of those rules is that the bishop and the elders have the authority to determine when someone is breaking them."

"So, following the rules mean being okay with what Sadie does because the church leaders say it's okay."

"Exactly."

"And if they had said she was in the wrong?"

"I would have agreed. I trust them. That's part of being Amish. We trust the leaders appointed over us to make *gut* decisions for us."

Vernon let out a long, slow breath. "So, you're okay if Sadie stays with us?"

"*Ya*. If she wants to stay. I understand if she wants to leave now. She might not see that what I did was out of concern for her."

"You could have spoken to her first."

"It seemed best to go straight to Amos. I don't take chances when it comes to breaking the *Ordnung*."

"*Oll recht*. I understand." Vernon stood up. He started to head for the door, then turned back. "Are we okay now, Arleta?" The question hung in the air.

She looked up from the ball of yarn in her hand. A stream of evening sunlight filtered in from the edge of the green blind and highlighted her features. Vernon could see the vulnerability in her expression, just like when they were children, before life had hardened her. *"Ya."* Her voice was quiet but powerful. "We are."

Chapter Fourteen

Sadie had been exhausted the night before, wrung out by all that had happened. She had collapsed onto her mattress and fallen into a deep sleep, even though she had tried to stay awake to hear how Vernon's conversation with Arleta had gone.

That deep sleep had not lasted long, however, and Sadie had spent a restless night tossing and turning in the sticky July air. Now the worries that had tormented her in the night returned as soon as she opened her eyes. Would her father still be upset with her, even though the church leaders had decided she wasn't breaking the *Ordnung*? Would he make her come home even earlier now? And what if he allowed her to stay? Surely Arleta would force her to leave. It was clear she wanted Sadie gone.

But how could she leave the children? They still needed her. And Vernon… The feelings were too overwhelming. After he supported and defended her last night, she was sure that he would want to court her. But what if Arleta kept them apart? And what would her father think? Vernon was eleven years older and known for putting distance between himself and the community. No, her father would never approve.

It seemed impossible for them to ever walk out together. Sadie's only hope was that Vernon's conversation with

Arleta had gone well the previous evening. She had not seen either of them before falling asleep—Arleta had gone to bed early and Vernon had gone out to check on potential flooding in the north field—so she could barely wait to hear what had happened between them. Her heart skipped a beat as she dared to believe that maybe, just maybe…

Sadie threw off the sheet and sat up. As she hurried to change into a purple cape dress, she heard the clip-clop of hooves in the driveway and the slow grind of wooden wheels on gravel. Vernon must have brought Big Red and the horse-drawn tractor out of the barn already. But then there was a knock on the front door.

Sadie frowned as she fastened her *kapp* in place. So that hadn't been Vernon in the yard? Who could be here at this hour? She grabbed her apron and tied the strings behind her back as she trotted through the *dawdi haus* parlor in her bare feet. There was another loud knock on the door. "Coming!" she said as she pulled the knot tight on her apron string, then smoothed the front of her dress.

Sadie opened the door to see her father standing on the porch with a stern look on his face.

She inhaled sharply. She knew he was concerned, but she had not expected him to show up on her doorstep first thing this morning.

"I've *kumme* to take you home." Abram's face showed that there would be no arguing his decision. But Sadie had to try.

"You agreed I could stay until the end of the month."

"That was before I knew that Vernon was sweet on you."

Sadie froze.

"You didn't think I'd notice?"

"It isn't like that. We're not courting. I promise." She felt exposed standing on the porch in the morning chill, her feelings for Vernon out in the open.

"You will be soon enough, if I don't intervene."

Sadie swallowed hard. She knew it would be a lie to contradict him. If Sadie had her way, Vernon would already be courting her.

"Get your belongings and let's go."

Sadie hesitated but knew there was nothing she could say.

"Right now, Sadie. You've just been in trouble for painting. Now you're living on the same farm with a man who wants to court you? It isn't seemly."

"I live in the *dawdi haus*. Arleta chaperones. She never breaks a rule."

"*Ya*. I can see that about her. But still, it isn't *oll recht* for you to stay here." Abram shook his head. "I don't approve of Vernon. He's too reclusive. It's like he's got something to hide. A *gut* Amish man shouldn't keep to himself like that."

"It's more complicated than that, *Daed*."

Abram snorted. "Everything seems complicated when you're young. When you're older, you realize it's not so hard to see things for the way they are." His eyes bore into hers. "It's just that you don't want to have to see it."

Sadie's hands shook. There was so much she wanted to explain, but couldn't.

"Go on, now. Get your suitcase. Your *mamm* expects us home for breakfast."

Sadie felt the fight drain from her. She knew her father would win the argument in the end. She turned and fled to her room before her father could see the hot, wet tears pricking her eyes. Her face stung as she folded her spare dress and apron and gathered her Bible, hairbrush and box of art supplies. Her father stood in the doorway, impatiently tapping his foot.

"*Oll recht*," Sadie said as she fastened the buckles on her old brown suitcase. "I'm ready. I just need to tell Vernon what's happening."

"Nee," Abram said. "I'll take care of that. You go to the buggy. It's parked out front."

"But I have to say goodbye to the *kinner*!"

"They aren't your concern anymore."

Tears blurred Sadie's vision as she waited in the buggy, her suitcase at her feet. It was all she could do not to jump from her seat, run to Vernon and tell him what she wanted to say. Her heart thudded in her ears, whispering a tight rhythm that sounded like *run-to-him, run-to-him, run-to-him.* Sadie squeezed her eyes shut and clenched her fists.

She heard heavy footsteps cut across the front yard. Her eyes flew open to see her father marching toward her. She glanced up at the farmhouse windows, searching for Vernon's face. Every pane of glass was covered by an opaque green blind. Was he going to let her go without saying goodbye?

Sadie kept her eyes on the front door of the big, weather-beaten farmhouse as the buggy pulled away, but Vernon did not appear. She craned her neck around, convinced that he would come after her, but the front door stayed firmly shut. Finally, as the buggy pulled onto the narrow country road, Sadie gave up.

The day passed, and still Sadie did not hear from Vernon. Each hour at home was packed with activity, which should have distracted her, but thoughts of Vernon and his children filled her head. As she watched her younger siblings, cooked and cleaned alongside her mother, Sadie's chest stayed tight with apprehension.

Her mind was on Vernon when a plate slipped from her hand and crashed onto the kitchen floor while cleaning up from the evening meal.

"Ach, Sadie, you're just not yourself anymore." Ada's eyes looked sad as she crouched down beside her daughter. "Let me help."

"Danki."

The spacious farmhouse kitchen felt unusually quiet as they collected the broken shards of porcelain. The baby sat in a high chair nibbling Cheerios. Sadie's other siblings were outside, helping with the chores under the supervision of their second oldest sister. The happy shouts of children carried through the open windows on the warm July breeze.

"You've barely smiled since you've been home," Ada said. "Are you missing the Kauffman *kinner*?"

"Ya. It's *gut* to see my own family again, but those *kinner* need me more."

Ada nodded thoughtfully. "And perhaps you're missing more than just the *kinner*?"

"Ach, well, Arleta and I didn't get on very well. She never wanted me there. But I thought we had managed to form a friendship. We ended up having some *gut* times together until…"

"That must have hurt for her to turn you over to the church elders."

Sadie sighed as she picked up the last shard of porcelain. "I didn't see it coming. I knew she didn't approve, but I didn't expect her to try to get me shunned."

Ada stood up, stretched her back and walked to the counter. "Maybe that wasn't her intention." She picked up a dishrag, dipped it in the soapy dishwater and wrung it out. "She may have seen it differently."

"Everyone sees things differently than I do."

Ada frowned as she crossed the kitchen. She remained silent as she crouched back down and wiped the floor with the damp dishrag.

"Sometimes I'm not sure I belong in Bluebird Hills, *Mamm*. I thought I had found a place for myself at Vernon's but now…" Sadie held up her hands in a pleading gesture. "What am I supposed to do? Who is going to understand me now?"

Ada's attention jerked from the floor to Sadie. "Sounds like you're missing more than just Arleta and the *kinner*."

Sadie studied the cracks in the worn wooden floorboards. "Vernon and I became friends," she said softly. "He understood me."

Ada sighed. "That's what your *daed* was afraid of."

"*Mamm*, we never broke a single rule. We're not walking out together. We're just friends. And Arleta was always there to chaperone, anyway."

Ada stood up and brushed off her apron. "There's more to it than that though, ain't so?"

Sadie pushed herself up from the floor. "What do you mean?"

"You and Vernon…" Ada's face tightened. "It's not a suitable match."

"Why not?"

"Your *daed* thinks he's too reclusive, too set in his ways. He's not a *gut* match for you."

"That's changing. Since I've been there, he's been healing from his loss. He's been going out. He's finding his way again."

Ada nodded. "I noticed that he stayed after church to visit and he went around Bluebird Hills last visiting Sunday."

"*Ya.*"

"You have a *gut* heart, Sadie. You've made a difference and helped that family." Ada pushed a loose strand of salt-and-pepper hair beneath her *kapp*. "But that doesn't mean you should stay with them any longer. You've done your job. Maybe it's time to move on now."

"But if Vernon is becoming a part of the community again, then what's the problem?"

"It's more than that," a deep voice said from the doorway.

Sadie flinched. She hadn't realized her father was listening.

"Vernon has always been a little different." He stood in the threshold of the kitchen with a serious expression on his face.

"Like me?" Sadie raised her eyebrows. She hoped her father would understand that being different in a homogenous community brought her and Vernon together.

"He's strong-willed like you, that's for certain sure. But he isn't like you, Sadie. He's too old for you and too hard. He's never been friendly, even before the accident. I don't understand what you see in him."

"Maybe he's not as stern as you think."

"His own sister turned you in to the bishop, ain't so? Do you think he's that different from his own sister? Do you really think he would value you for who you are?"

"*Ya*. I do." Sadie's fists clenched by her sides. "He understands me."

"*Ach*, Sadie." A flicker of sadness passed over Abram's weather-beaten face. His frown lines looked even deeper than usual. "You're so young and naive. You trust everyone. You have so much to learn about the world."

"Maybe Vernon *is* trustworthy. Maybe there is more to him than you see on the surface."

"You know a tree by its fruits."

"But I've seen the fruits, *Daed*, and they're *gut*!"

Abram looked thoughtful and Sadie thought she might

have persuaded him. But, after a moment, he shook his head. "Give it time, *dochder.* Go to more singings and youth group gatherings. Find a *gut bu* your age who won't try to stop you from being yourself."

"But I *am* myself around Vernon." Sadie's heart thudded into her throat. She had to make her father see. Why did he refuse to understand? "He's the first person who's ever really understood me!"

Abram looked at her with sad eyes. "I know this is hard for you to understand, Sadie, but I'm protecting you. I'm doing what's best for you. I know you better than you think, and I don't believe that Vernon sees you the way you think he does."

Sadie shook her head so hard her *kapp* strings bounced against her cheeks. "That's not true, *Daed.* He sees me for who I really am! And I think... I think he loves me for it."

Silence fell over the kitchen. Ada stood with wide, unblinking eyes, as if something unbelievable had just occurred. Abram sucked in a sharp intake of breath. A hard mask slid over his face. "I don't want you leaving the house, Sadie. Not until you're out from under his spell. You're not thinking straight. Some time with your family will set you straight. Then you'll get back to your regular life, meet a nice *bu*..."

"*Daed*, I can't stay shut up here, stuck in the house. What if Vernon needs me? And what about the *kinner*? I didn't even get to say goodbye."

Abram's eyes were still sad behind that hard mask. "Sadie," he said gently, the harshness in his voice gone. "He knows where you live. He hasn't *kumme* to say goodbye. He hasn't *kumme* to check on you. He's letting you go."

"You don't think he cares for me at all." Sadie fought the sharp prickle of tears behind her eyes.

"I think he's a complicated man, Sadie. I don't think he knows how to love a girl like you."

Abram's words rang in Sadie's ears the rest of the night. By the next afternoon, she began to give up hope. Her ears still strained to hear the clip-clop of Old Max's hooves and the grind of wagon wheels over gravel, but her heart was heavy. Maybe her father was right. Vernon could have easily come after her by now.

Maybe he didn't want to.

The racket of five children in the room beneath her bedroom woke Sadie the next morning. She dressed quickly as she listened to the bangs and shouts vibrating the wooden floorboards beneath her bare feet. Her childhood home was so loud and rambunctious that it was almost a distraction from her worries. *Almost.* She loved seeing her family again, but the sharp ache in her chest would not go away. She had begun to feel at home at the Kauffman farm, as though it were more than just a place to work. She even missed Ned's and Newt's ridiculous antics.

There was a loud pounding of footsteps in the hallway, then her bedroom door flew open. Three of her younger siblings spilled into the room, all shouting at once. "You've got company! *Kumme* fast before *Daed* makes them leave! He doesn't look happy."

Sadie gasped and flew out of her bedroom, her *kapp* askew and her apron strings unevenly tied. Her feet pounded down the stairs behind her siblings. She rushed through the entry hall and out the front door to see Vernon standing opposite her father on the porch, staring at one another awkwardly. Before she could catch her breath, Ned, Newt and Lydia flew at her in a rush of hugs and shouts.

"We missed you!" the boys said as they wrapped their

arms around her. She grinned as she felt their sticky hands on the back of her neck. Lydia pulled at her dress until Sadie crouched down and hugged her too. She breathed in the sweet scent of children's shampoo, closed her eyes and smiled.

"Please *kumme* back, Sadie." Lydia's breath felt hot on Sadie's cheek. "It's not the same without you."

Sadie's heart flooded with warmth. But when she opened her eyes and looked up, her father was staring down at her with his usual stern expression. Sadie forced herself to let go of the children and stand up. "Go play while the grownups talk. My sister Anna will look after you." The boys dashed away to join Sadie's brothers in the yard. Lydia was a bit more reluctant, but Anna tempted her with a freshly baked snickerdoodle. Soon the front porch was empty except for Vernon, Sadie and her parents.

Abram kept his eyes on Vernon, an unmistakably disapproving expression on his face. Ada wrung her hands as she glanced back and forth between the two men. Sadie wanted to run to Vernon as he stood there, silent and strong. But, with her father watching, she did nothing but stare. The pulse on her throat fluttered as she fought to stay still.

"*Kumme* and sit," Ada said after the long, awkward pause. "I'll get *kaffi* and snickerdoodles."

"They haven't *kumme* for *kaffi* and cookies," Abram growled as he slumped into one of the wooden rocking chairs that lined the porch. Ada settled nervously onto the edge of her rocker. She looked like she might jump up at any moment. The laughter of children carried in the humid air alongside the buzz of insect wings. Beyond the porch lay a patchwork of green and yellow fields planted with summer crops.

"We want Sadie to *kumme* back," Vernon said after everyone had settled into a chair and the tension was almost too much to bear. He maintained eye contact with Abram without looking away, despite the fiery disapproval in Abram's unflinching gaze.

"Of course you do," Ada jumped in. "She's a *gut* girl, but—"

"Let's get to the point," Abram cut in. "What are your intentions with our Sadie?" Abram's eyes narrowed and he leaned forward in his chair.

Sadie's heart caught in her throat as she waited for Vernon's answer. The silence pounded in her ears in time with her pulse. Vernon's eyes slid to hers and she nodded. He returned the nod, then looked back at Abram. "I don't want her to *kumme* back as a *kinnsmaad*. I want her to *kumme* back as my wife. I love her."

Sadie could not comprehend what she had just heard. She shot up from her chair. "You want to marry me?" Her lip quivered, then broke into an irrepressible grin. Suddenly, there was no one on the porch but her and Vernon. "When you didn't say goodbye or *kumme* after me..."

"I was already in the fields when your *Daed* came to get you. Arleta had gotten up early to watch the *kinner* so you could rest after what you'd been through the day before. I would never have let you leave without saying goodbye— or trying to stop you."

He stood up and faced her, his expression mirroring hers. Sadie had never seen him smile so big before. She had not even known it was possible. He was beaming—actually beaming with joy. She knew he was feeling exactly what she was feeling. "I love you," he said in a deep, gentle voice. "And I want to marry you."

Nothing existed but her and the man she loved—the man who loved her in return.

It had been love all along—from the first moment she

had gazed into his unyielding eyes and seen the man who lay beneath the mask.

"Sit down and be reasonable." Abram's harsh voice jerked Sadie from her moment of joy. Her attention lurched from Vernon to her father. "I love him too, *Daed*," she said in a desperate whisper. Hearing herself say it out loud for the first time felt right, and she knew it was true.

"You're the prettiest girl in Bluebird Hills," Abram said, his voice rising. "Of course he's fallen in love with you. But he doesn't really know you, Sadie. This won't last."

"Abram, I understand how you feel—"

"You have no idea how I feel." Abram stood up from his chair to face Vernon.

Vernon paused, then started over. "*Ya*, everyone knows Sadie's the prettiest girl around. I can see that, same as everyone else. But that isn't why I'm in love with her."

Abram snorted.

"Let's all sit down and talk about this calmly," Ada said. "I'll get the *kaffi*. We can work this out."

"*Kaffi* won't solve this," Abram said. But he sat back down, as Ada had asked. Vernon and Sadie followed suit. Ada shifted nervously in her chair instead of getting up to fetch refreshments.

Vernon took a deep breath, then let the words flow. "Sadie isn't like anyone else I've ever met. It's her heart that has captured me. She has a goodness inside of her that can't be hidden. You can see it in the way her eyes sparkle, in the way she's always laughing, in the way she worked so hard to reach my *kinner* and my sister…and me." Vernon swallowed hard. "I was a hard man when Sadie arrived. I wanted to be left alone to be miserable and angry. I felt so guilty about the buggy accident that destroyed my family that I couldn't face anyone. But Sadie showed me there was still life to be lived.

She's so full of life and joy that it overflowed onto me and my entire family. She has a way of seeing the world that's special and she taught me to see it that way too. Her painting, her creativity—it all captured me. I love her for who she is and for how she thinks, not just for how she looks."

Vernon flexed his jaw and looked away. Sadie could tell those words had cost him dearly. Only love could have motivated him to spill his secrets—and in front of Abram Lapp, of all people.

There was a long silence. Ned's voice drifted across the yard, followed by distant laughter. Cicadas hummed and Ada's chair creaked as she rocked. Sadie could feel sweat forming beneath her *kapp* and behind her knees.

Abram ran his fingers through his long gray beard as he stared at Vernon. Sadie knew he was considering every word Vernon had said. "You love her for how she thinks?"

"*Ya*, I do."

"Explain."

"Uh, well…" Vernon removed his straw hat and set it on his knees. He wiped the moisture from his forehead with his hand. "She doesn't think like anyone else. Knowing her has been a journey into a new world, without ever leaving home. She's creative and she isn't afraid to follow that creative spirit. She taught my *kinner* to paint. I guess you know that, since she ended up having to defend herself to the church leaders. I defended her too. Because she used that creativity to reach and heal my family. I know that her creativity has been controversial—we've all heard the complaints over the years that she's too different, that she doesn't follow our ways closely enough. But I support her. I've seen how her creativity is her way of reaching *Gott*—and helping others reach Him too." Vernon shook his head. "I know it doesn't make sense, but it's what I've seen and I won't back down from that. I don't expect you to understand."

Abram released a long, slow breath and leaned back in his chair. "I do understand. That's why I've been so concerned."

Sadie sat up straighter. "What?"

"Our Sadie has always been different." Abram kept his eyes on Vernon, still sizing him up, but with less animosity now. "From the time she was a little *maedel,* she saw the world differently. I saw how *gut* and sweet her heart was—and I knew that heart needed to be protected. As she grew older, I saw that men would want to court her for her looks, but would never be able to understand her. If she married a man like that, he would crush her spirit eventually. I couldn't let that happen."

Sadie's mouth hung open. She could not comprehend what her father was saying. "All these years, you were trying to…protect me?"

Abram lowered his brows as if it were obvious. "*Ya,* of course. I've been trying to protect your free spirit."

"But I thought you wanted to crush that in me!"

Abram's expression softened. "Crush? Never." He shook his head sadly. "But there's no place for a *maedel* like you among the Amish. I had to teach you how to survive as one of us, for your own *gut.*" Abram grunted. "And Vernon, well, he seemed like the worst match possible for you. He's hard and set in his ways. The kind of man who would eventually crush the spirit of a woman like you, Sadie. Can't you see why I had to force you apart?"

"I hope I've proven otherwise," Vernon said.

"Proven?" Abram sighed. "You've said the right things, that's for certain sure. But proven?" He shook his head. "*Nee,* words are easily said. They can mean nothing."

"Then how about I show you?" Vernon stood up, his excitement evident in the suddenness of his movements.

"Show me what?"

Vernon grinned. "*Kumme* with me, all of you, and you'll see."

Vernon, Arleta, Sadie and her parents stood in front of the Kauffman barn. Ned and Newt jumped up and down, while Lydia clung to Sadie's hand and pulled her forward. Sadie's siblings had stayed at the Lapp farmhouse, where Anna could watch them. The Kauffman children had insisted on coming, shouting that they had helped with the surprise. Sadie's anticipation had grown throughout the buggy ride, until she was about to burst. Now the time had come.

Vernon eased the big double doors open and the earthy smell of oats and mud rose to meet them. Sunshine streamed inside, highlighting the dust motes drifting in the still, hot air. "Follow me." Vernon walked quickly, excitement and nerves driving his steps. They passed the row of stalls, then turned the corner toward the tack room. But instead of empty storage space beside the tack room, there was a wall and a closed door. The bales of hay, bags of feed corn and old rusted farm equipment were gone, replaced by new construction.

"Where did this wall come from?" Sadie asked. She grinned and looked at Vernon. "What have you been up to?"

He gave a sheepish shrug and motioned her to open the door. Lydia tugged Sadie forward and the twins knocked into her as they crowded toward the doorway.

"One, two, three, open!" the twins shouted. Sadie flung open the door to reveal an art studio tucked behind the new wallboard. There was a big easel in the middle of the room, a table with four folding chairs and shelves stocked with art supplies. A window let in plenty of light from a blue summer sky.

Sadie gasped. "It's *wunderbar*!"

"We knew you'd like it!" Newt shouted.

Ned jumped up and down as he added, "I picked out the easel!"

"And I hammered some of the nails to put up the wall!" Newt said.

"Me too!" Ned said.

"I handed *Daed* the tools when he asked for them," Lydia said.

"It's why we didn't *kumme* to get you sooner," Ned said. "*Daed* said we had to show you how much we appreciate you first."

Sadie was too stunned to respond. She stood, taking it all in, feeling more seen and heard than she had ever thought possible.

"I hope it makes you happy, Sadie," Vernon said softly.

"Happier than I can say."

He reached for her hand and squeezed. Sadie felt complete, holding his big, calloused hand in the room he had made just for her, so she could be herself.

Vernon looked over at Abram, but kept Sadie's hand tightly in his. "I hope you see how I feel now. I want Sadie to use the gifts *Gott* gave her. I don't want to crush her creativity. I want to encourage it."

Abram grunted as he stroked his long gray beard. "*Ya*. I can see that." He shook his head and chuckled. "You're full of surprises, Vernon. I had you wrong. I admit it and I give you and Sadie my blessing to marry."

Ada looked at Sadie with shining eyes. "I'm happy for you, Sadie."

"But even though you have my blessing, there is still a potential problem," Abram said.

Sadie's heart skipped a beat as her attention jerked to her father. "What, *Daed*?"

"Arleta. How do you feel about all this?" Abram swept his hand over the room. "You turned Sadie in for church discipline. Are you going to keep fighting my *dochder*? She needs a sister-in-law who will support her."

Arleta stood in the threshold, watching everyone. They all turned at once to see her reaction. "I did what a *gut* Amish friend should do. I didn't report her out of animosity, but out of concern." She shrugged. "The bishop and the elders say her art is *oll recht*, so it's *oll recht*. Now that we know that, I don't mind if she paints with the *kinner*."

"But…" Sadie knitted her brows together, trying to understand Arleta's logic.

"Part of following the rules is trusting the people who make them. So if the church leaders approve, so do I."

Sadie rushed to Arleta and wrapped her in an energetic hug. Arleta laughed nervously and patted Sadie's back. "Don't worry, Sadie, we're going to be friends. I appreciate what you've done for us. I don't like needing help, but I do appreciate that you've given it." Arleta peeled away from Sadie's hug. "But I'm never going to become a hugger. We can be friends without all that."

The room erupted in laughter. "That's our Arleta," Vernon said.

"*I* want hugs!" Lydia tugged at the skirt of Sadie's dress.

"Then you can have all you want, because I'm going to stay here with you from now on."

Vernon stepped closer. He put his hands on her shoulders and gazed deep into her eyes. "Does this mean you'll marry me?"

"Ya." She smiled. "Of course I'll marry you. You understand me, Vernon, like no one else ever could. I love you for it—and for so much more."

Vernon wrapped her in a hug, with Lydia between them. Then Ned and Newt joined in, jostling for space. Love filled the room to bursting and Sadie knew she was where she truly belonged, surrounded by the people who truly loved her.

Epilogue

The Kauffman family gathered in their favorite space—Sadie's art studio. Vernon watched his newlywed wife as she stood at the easel, brow creased in concentration, her paintbrush flying over the canvas in a vibrant swirl of colors. He smiled inside. "You're painting our farm, aren't you?"

Sadie stopped and looked over her shoulder at him. "How can you tell? I've barely begun. It's mostly just colors."

"I can tell because I know how you think." He studied the kaleidoscope of yellows, golds and greens. "Those are colors of happiness and home." He leaned forward and pointed to a block of color. "And that's the farmhouse, ain't so?"

"It's going to be."

Vernon nodded. "You've captured how it feels, not how it looks."

"Exactly."

Lydia wrinkled her nose as she sat at the table with a fat Magic Marker in her hand. "How does a house feel?"

Sadie scanned the room. "It feels like love."

Arleta and the twins groaned. "Enough of that," Arleta said as she rolled her eyes.

Sadie flashed a playful grin. "You know it's true."

Arleta waved her hand dismissively, but her smile gave her away.

"Why don't you show us what you can do?" Sadie asked.

Arleta hesitated, then gave a decisive nod. "*Oll recht.* It's my turn."

Sadie took a few minutes to move her canvas from the easel and set up Arleta with a fresh Mason jar of water, clean brushes and a blank canvas. Arleta put on one of the old aprons hanging from a peg on the wall. She picked up a brush and stared for a moment, then shrugged. "I don't see what all the fuss is about, but I'll give it a try…" She didn't move though.

"*Aenti* Arleta, it won't paint itself," Lydia said.

"*Ach*, I don't know how."

"Feel everything inside you—all the emotions you've got stored up, bursting to break free—and let them pour out," Sadie said. "Don't think. Just do it."

"Humph," Arleta muttered, but she dipped her paintbrush in gray paint and began to attack the canvas. Soon, she was splattering paint everywhere, flicking and throwing it from her brush, until fat drops of paint covered the canvas—and the surrounding floor.

The rest of the family looked up from their art projects to watch. Arleta rinsed the gray paint from the brush, dipped it in yellow paint then began flicking it at the canvas again.

Vernon started to say something, but Sadie put a hand on his arm and shook her head. "Don't interrupt," she whispered. "She needs to do this."

"Even though it's making such a mess?" Vernon whispered back. "Paint is splattering everywhere."

"It's *oll recht.* That's why you built this studio. It doesn't matter if she makes a mess in here. This is how she needs to get her emotions out."

"You're right." Vernon put his arm around his wife and drew her to his side as they watched Arleta create her own unique art.

"There," Arleta said after just a few minutes. "All finished."

"That was fast," Newt said.

Ned squinted at the yellow and gray splattered canvas. "What is it?"

"It's obvious," Arleta said.

"Only to you," Newt said as he tilted his head for an alternative view.

"All that gray is how I used to feel, shut up in the *dawdi haus* after the accident, frustrated and lonely. There's a layer of yellow on top because that's how I feel these days, mostly at least. Things are brighter. But the gray's still there because it still isn't easy. I have a lot of rehabilitation left to do."

"You've *kumme* a long way with the *Englisch* therapist," Vernon said. He had never been so relieved as when Arleta finally agreed to go back for regular sessions at the rehabilitation center in Lancaster.

Arleta nodded. "So the gray isn't there as much. *Gott* has replaced it with yellow. And He's given me the ability to cope with the parts of my life that still feel gray."

Sadie studied the painting. "*Ya.* I can see that. It's all right there."

Newt made a face. "The only thing I see there is a bunch of spilled paint."

Arleta chuckled. "Well, I don't expect to see it in a museum. I'm no artist. This painting was just for me, and you know what? I actually do feel better now." She shook her head. "How strange."

"I knew it would help!" Sadie's face broke into a big grin.

"And don't be so sure you're not an artist. You should see what *Englishers* put in their art museums. There's a famous painter who dripped and splattered paint to create his art. Those paintings sell for millions."

Arleta grunted. "Well, there's no accounting for those *lecherich Englisch* ideas." She stared at her painting for a moment then turned to Sadie with a skeptical expression. "Is that really true?"

"*Ya*, even if it does sound like a ridiculous idea to you. His name is Jackson Pollock."

"Huh." Arleta looked amused, and perhaps even a bit pleased with her artwork.

"We can check out a book of his paintings from the library and I'll show you."

"*Nee*," Arleta set down her paintbrush. "No need for *lecherich Englisch* paintings in this *haus*. Between all of you, we've got enough ridiculousness here as it is."

Vernon thought Arleta might be irritated, but when he looked at her, he realized she was teasing. He grinned at her.

"Well," Sadie said, "what if I told you there is about to be another *lecherich* artist in this family?"

It took Vernon a few beats to register what Sadie was saying. Then his mouth dropped open. "You mean…"

Sadie beamed. "That's right, Vernon. We're going to have a *boppli*."

Vernon's emotions exploded into joy. He rushed for Sadie, picked her up and spun her around in the air. "Our *bobbli* is going to be a *wunderbar* artist, just like you." He set Sadie back on her feet and she clung to him, laughing as she regained her balance.

Arleta put her hands on her hips and raised an eyebrow at Vernon. "Or this *bobbli* might take after the *aenti*, and enjoy rules and traditions, instead of being a free spirit."

"Either way, this *boppli* will be perfect." Vernon looked around at his wife, children and sister and knew that his life had overflowed with redemption he never thought possible. "*Gott* makes everyone different and there is room for all of those differences in this family."

"Even when it seems impossible," Sadie added.

"Especially then." Vernon nodded as he placed a hand over his wife's belly, imagining the new life forming within and the new promises waiting to be revealed.

* * * * *

If you liked this story from Virginia Wise,
check out her previous Love Inspired books:

The Secret Amish Admirer
An Amish Christmas Inheritance

Available now from Love Inspired!
Find more great reads at
www.LoveInspired.com.

Dear Reader,

I have been looking forward to sharing Sadie's story with you ever since she first appeared in book #1 of the Bluebird Hills series as an artist trying to forge her way in a community that did not always recognize her value. I am so glad that she has finally gotten the happily-ever-after she deserves. Thank you for returning to Bluebird Hills to see her find love and bring healing to others by embracing who God made her to be. I hope that we can all find the courage to use the gifts God has given us, just like Sadie does.

And I hope you'll join me again for the next happily-ever-after in Bluebird Hills' tightknit Amish community. Favorite, familiar characters will be back next time, along with new ones that I'm eager for you to meet. In the meantime, you can find me at virginiawisebooks.com, Facebook @VirginiaWiseBooks, and Instagram @virginiawisebooks. I'd love to connect with you there.

Love Always,
Virginia

HARLEQUIN
Reader Service

Enjoyed your book?

Try the perfect subscription for Romance readers and get more great books like this delivered right to your door.

See why over 10+ million readers have tried Harlequin Reader Service.

Start with a Free Welcome Collection with free books and a gift—valued over $20.

Choose any series in print or ebook. See website for details and order today:

TryReaderService.com/subscriptions

RSBPA24R